HALF·MOON
INVESTIGATIONS

OTHER BOOKS BY EOIN COLFER

HALF·MOON
INVESTIGATIONS

EOIN COLFER

MIRAMAX BOOKS
Hyperion Paperbacks for Children
New York

Text copyright © 2006 by Eoin Colfer
All rights reserved. No part of this book may be reproduced or
transmitted in any form or by any means, electronic or mechanical,
including photocopying, recording, or by any information storage
and retrieval system, without written permission from the publisher.
For information address
Hyperion Books for Children, 114 Fifth Avenue,
New York, New York 10011-5690.

First U.S. paperback edition, 2007
1 3 5 7 9 10 8 6 4 2
Printed in the United States of America
ISBN-13: 978-0-7868-4960-4
ISBN-10: 0-7868-4960-6

Love Me Tender
Words and Music by Elvis Presley and Vera Matson
Copyright © 1956 by Elvis Presley Music, Inc.
Copyright Renewed and Assigned to Elvis Presley Music
All Rights Administered by Cherry River Music Co. and Chrysalis Songs
International Copyright Secured
All Rights Reserved

To All the Girls I've Loved Before
Lyric by Hal David
Music by Albert Hammond
Copyright © 1975 (Renewed 2003), 1984 EMI APRIL MUSIC INC.
and CASA DAVID
All Rights Reserved
International Copyright Secured
Used by Permission

Visit www.hyperionbooksforchildren.com

To Liam and John:
The Thursday-Night Think Tank

THE FIRST RULE OF INVESTIGATION

MY NAME IS MOON. Fletcher Moon. And I'm a private detective. In my twelve years on this spinning ball we call Earth, I've seen a lot of things normal people never see. I've seen lunch boxes stripped of everything except fruit. I've seen counterfeit homework networks that operated in five counties, and I've seen truckloads of candy taken from babies.

I thought I'd seen it all. I had paid so many visits to the gutter looking for lost valentines, that I thought nothing could shock me. After all, when you've come face-to-face with the dark side of the school yard, life doesn't hold many surprises.

Or so I believed. I was wrong. Very wrong.

One month ago a case came knocking on my

door that made me consider getting out of the detective business for good. I'd just turned twelve, and already I had a dozen successful investigations under my belt. Business was good, but I was ready to start solving actual crimes. No more kid stuff. I wanted real cases that paid real money, not just whatever a kid happened to have in his pocket at the time.

It all went wrong the day I decided to break Bob Bernstein's first rule of investigation: *Be invisible. Put the pieces of the puzzle together, but never become one of those pieces yourself.*

Herod Sharkey made me forget that rule.

As every private investigator knows, Bob Bernstein is the legendary FBI agent turned PI, who founded the Bernstein Academy in Washington, D.C., to train aspiring investigators properly. He also wrote the Bernstein manual, which every student needs to know by heart if they are to have any hope of qualifying. I knew the manual from cover to cover, and I had qualified at the top of my online class, though I'd had to use my dad's birth certificate to do it. Luckily we both share the same name.

September twenty-seventh. That day is as clear to me as a high-resolution photograph. The end of our first month back in school after the summer holidays. Unfortunately the summer didn't know it was over and was pouring on the sunshine. The heat came off the tar concrete in sheets, wrapping itself around the students of Saint Jerome's Elementary and Middle School.

I arrived at the gates around the usual time, 8:50. I like to be ten minutes early wherever I'm going. Gives me time to get my finger on whatever pulse is beating. Private detectives need to be in touch with their environment. The Bernstein manual says that *A detective never knows where his next case is coming from.* For all he knows, it could be a puzzle that he has already solved, if he's kept his eyes open. So I keep my eyes wide open. I can tell you which kids have wart acid on their fingers. I know who's passing lovey-dovey notes around in the yard, and even which teachers stop off at the Burger Mac on their way to school.

But nobody can possibly see everything. Not even the legendary detective Bob Bernstein. That's why I needed my informants. Doobie Doyle was the best one I had. An eight-year-old snot-nosed snitch with sharp eyes and a big mouth. Doobie would sell out his own mother for a sweaty handful of jelly beans. Unfortunately, when I say Doobie was snot-nosed, it's not just a turn of phrase. Doobie never went anywhere without a couple of green yo-yo's hanging from his nostrils, which he then snorted back up so hard that they wrapped around his brain. Actually, it was the perfect disguise. It was all people noticed about him. If Doobie ever wiped his nose, his own mother wouldn't be able to pick him out of a lineup.

On that morning, the twenty-seventh, he was at

the gates waiting for me. I was surprised. Usually I had to track him down. This must be important.

"Morning, Fletcher," he said, trotting along beside me.

I didn't look down. A close-up view of Doobie was not how you wanted to start your day.

"What have you got for me?" I asked casually.

"Did you see *Captain Laserbeam* last night? There was a mud monster."

Doobie was a good snitch, but he distracted easily.

"Let's talk about cartoons later, Doobie. Do you have some information?"

"Yep. Good stuff. But I want to see the badge."

I sighed. Doobie always wanted to see the badge. It was shiny, and he was eight.

"Okay. One peek, then spill the beans."

I reached into my pants pocket and pulled out a small leather wallet. I flipped it in front of Doobie's face. Inside was a laminated card and a silver-plated detective's badge. Sunlight winked along the badge's ridges, and for a long moment I was mesmerized by it. Even after six months, I sometimes found it hard to believe that it was finally mine.

"Wow," said Doobie, with real reverence, which gave way quickly to doubt. "You sure this is real?"

I tapped the laminated card. "It's all right there, Doobie. Fletcher Moon. Graduate of the Bob Bernstein Private Detective Academy."

"Can I have it?" asked Doobie, just like he did every time he saw the badge.

"No," I replied, slipping the wallet back into my pocket. "This took me two years to earn. Even if you had it, it wouldn't be yours."

Doobie frowned. This kind of thinking was a bit advanced for someone who hadn't yet worked out the mechanics of a tissue.

"So, what have you got for me, Doobie? Something juicy, I hope?"

"I dunno what I've got," he said. "I only came looking 'cause everyone knows I'm your secret snitch and they asked me to find you."

I stopped. "Who asked you?"

"Herod Sharkey," replied Doobie. "I don't know who the other one is, but he's big, really big."

Herod Sharkey. According to school yard rules, that name shouldn't have bothered me in the least. After all, I was in seventh grade and Herod was merely a fifth-grader. But the Sharkey family wasn't one for rules. In fact, if there *was* an unbroken rule somewhere, the Sharkeys would drive several hundred miles out of their way just to break it.

Herod was one of the school bad kids. The teachers have a name for people like Herod. They call him one of the "usual suspects." Whenever anything went missing, he was routinely summoned to the principal's office for questioning. Nine out of ten times, Herod had the missing thing in his pocket. The other time, he had probably buried it in the sports field. It wouldn't be long before the police began to call the school looking for him.

So why would Herod Sharkey be looking for me? I didn't own anything valuable. *Except my detective's badge.* My hand went instinctively to my pocket, but the wallet was still there. I decided to check it every thirty seconds or so, just to be on the safe side.

I dropped my bag off at my locker, then followed Doobie around the side of the school, past the oil tank that had been painted to look like Thomas the Tank Engine, to the basketball court, where all the major student business was conducted. If you needed to hire someone to tell someone that a third person liked them, then this was the place to find that someone. The basketball court was also the agreed location for school fights. I could see from the ragged ring of kids that someone had booked an early slot to settle a disagreement.

"Where's Herod?" I asked Doobie, though I already knew. Herod was a Sharkey, so there was only one place that he was likely to be.

"He's fighting. They're headlocked."

I nodded. Headlocked was better than pinwheeling. A person could get himself injured getting involved in a Pinwheel.

There are several kinds of school fights. The three most popular kinds are the Pinwheel, the

6

Hold-Me-Back, and the Headlock. In the Pinwheel, the two fighters run at each other, eyes closed and arms spinning. The object was to catch your opponent with a lucky shot, but more often than not the enemies missed each other by yards. The Pinwheel was popular with younger kids.

It could be argued that the Hold-Me-Back is not, strictly speaking, a fight at all, since the object is to avoid the conflict altogether. In a Hold-Me-Back, the opponents scream "Hold me back!" as loudly and often as possible until a teacher arrives to break things up. Following the adult's arrival, the secretly relieved opponents are led away by their friends, still shouting things like *You were lucky, butt face! I would have murdered you.*

The Headlock was what we were dealing with on that day. The Headlock does exactly what it says on the can. Two boys get each other in a mutual headlock, and whoever lets go first is the loser. Grip is everything in a Headlock. Some boys favor lacing the fingers, others go for the wrist grip. It depends really on length and strength of fingers. There are many reasons why the loser loses. Not being able to breathe is one, needing a bathroom break is another. There is a school-yard legend of two bitter enemies, Burton McHale and Jerry Canty, who stayed headlocked for twenty straight hours. Their friends brought them food, and they went to the bathroom without using the bathroom, if you see what I mean. Those who have tried this tactic say it is only embarrassing the first time.

I approached the circle around the fight, uncertain why my feet were carrying me forward. What could be here for a detective? I was not fond of violent situations. It wasn't that I'd never been in a fight, it was just that I'd never won one. But there was a stronger instinct driving me forward. I smelled a mystery. My detective's nose pulled me closer to the action. I could no more ignore this than a magpie could ignore a diamond ring on a windowsill.

Doobie elbowed his way through the crowd. "I got him. I got Moon."

The crowd parted, repelled by the sight of Doobie's nose. Nobody wanted to chance contact with those stringy greeners. I followed through to the eye of the hurricane. All eyes were on me, which was not how it was supposed to be. Detectives should never be in the thick of the action. We were supposed to turn up later and ask questions. The closest a detective gets to a bullet is dusting the shell casing for prints. And yet here I was, following an eight-year-old into the middle of a fight circle.

There were two figures in the center. One was Herod Sharkey, short and skinny with the signature Sharkey red hair. The other was not a boy, as Doobie had thought, it was Bella Barnes, the biggest kid in the school. Bella stood nearly six feet tall in her woolly stockings and played rugby on the boys' team.

Nobody messed with Bella. Ever. Not even the teachers. And yet, here was Herod Sharkey latched on to her back like a tick on a mutt.

I was stunned for a moment. Then I composed myself and took a mental snapshot of the scene, memorizing the details. According to the Bernstein manual: *A detective never knows which seemingly insignificant fact will solve the case.*

So. Details. Bella Barnes. Five eleven. Maybe two hundred pounds. Twelve and a half years old. Regulation school uniform, except for expressly forbidden dangling earrings, which could catch on a doorknob and rip a lobe, according to Mrs. Quinn, the school principal. Though nobody had ever seen or heard of this happening.

Then there was Herod Sharkey. Known as Roddy to his family, and not to be confused with his big brother Red. Four and a half feet tall, silver tracksuit, and brown hiking boots. Not school regulation, but the height of ten-year-old cool. Herod had his skinny arms wrapped around Bella's neck, and they were barely long enough to meet at the front. Strictly speaking, this was not a classic Headlock, as only one of the antagonists had a grip on the other.

Herod looked up from his struggle. His face was flushed but determined. A hush dropped like a blanket over the other kids, as they waited for the little Sharkey to speak. I had a feeling that whatever he said, I wouldn't like it.

"Moon, you nerd," said Herod.

So far, my feeling was right.

"You're the big detective. Prove to this hippo that I didn't take her organizer."

Bella bucked, tossing Herod like a rodeo jockey, but he held on grimly.

"You took it," rasped Bella. "April saw you."

"Barbie's lying! I didn't take nothing."

A delicate-looking girly-girl in the crowd pointed a finger at Herod.

"Double negative!" she squealed triumphantly. "You did it, Sharkey. I saw you. You and your brother have been stealing from us for years."

This was April Devereux, ten years old and already the head of an entire tribe of Barbies. Herod's description of her may not have been very politically correct, but it was accurate. If a Barbie doll walked through a magnification tunnel, April Devereux would emerge at the other end.

"You're lying!" shouted Herod. "And Half Moon will prove it."

I was wondering how long it would be before someone brought up my nickname. I had been christened Half Moon by Herod's brother, Red, back when I was in third grade. Even then I hadn't been the tallest stalk in the field.

"What do you expect me to do?" I asked him.

"You're always banging on about this famous detective badge. So detect something."

This was ridiculous. This was not how detectives worked.

"Go on, Fletcher," said April Devereux, managing to speak and pout at the same time. "Do us all a favor and prove I'm telling the truth."

I grimaced at the gathered crowd.

"What can I do? I don't have the facts. I wouldn't know where to begin."

Bella glared at me. "You better begin," she said hoarsely. "Or I'm going to roll over and crush this ant. Then I'm going to take your precious badge and stuff it somewhere painful."

I paled, but not as much as Herod did.

"Hurry, Moon," he said urgently. "If I get crushed, my family will come looking for you."

I felt as though I had wandered into somebody else's nightmare, but it was too late to back away slowly and close the dream door behind me. There were a hundred eyes on me, all expecting a rabbit out of a hat.

Doobie elbowed me. "Go on, Fletcher," he said. "You can do it."

I suspected that Doobie wanted me to enter the fray so that he could have my badge when I didn't come back.

April Devereux's gang of April clones stamped and pouted at me. It was quite unnerving. They generally looked so pink and harmless.

"I can't do anything here. You need a referee, not a detective."

Herod's forehead was pretty red now, with the effort of hanging on. "You better help, Half Moon. I'm warning you."

There was no point in arguing. You couldn't debate with Herod Sharkey. It would be as pointless as trying to sell a vegetarian lifestyle to a T. rex. The best thing to do would be to turn around and leave. So, I gave that a try, but the crowd was not as eager to let me out as it had been to let me in. I was an interesting wrinkle in an otherwise boring headlock fight. The kids surged forward, forcing me closer to the fight itself.

As I was bumped backward, I realized that I was in a very vulnerable position. All Herod had to do was scissor his legs.

Herod must have realized this too, for he suddenly kicked his skinny legs up and wrapped them around my neck. My balance was off, so I toppled to the ground, bouncing off Bella's thigh on the way down.

The other kids cheered. This was a positive development as far as they were concerned.

I was disgusted more than afraid. Herod was only ten, and small for his age, so he couldn't do much more than keep me on the ground—not in this position. But time was ticking on and soon the bell would ring, and Principal Quinn would make her way out here with her dogs, Larry and Adam, to see what the problem was. And the rules said that anyone caught in a fight paid a little visit to the office.

Herod's boot laces were wedged up under my chin, and his feet were hooked together. I tried to unwind them, but unfortunately I was one-handed. Bella had rolled over my right arm. It felt like I had been steamrolled. Surely my arm was cartoon flat.

"You better start thinking, Half Moon," said Herod. "Otherwise we're going down to the office together."

"Yeah, Half Moon," chimed in Bella. "Get your thinking cap on."

Apparently I was the bad guy now.

There was a simple solution. Simple but not very macho. However, I had little time and no options. With my free hand, I grabbed Herod's left heel and tugged off his hiking boot.

"Hey!" he shouted. "What are you doing? He's stealing my shoe."

I wasn't, of course, stealing his shoe. What I was doing was much less dignified. Before Herod could figure out what was going on, I grabbed his foot, and with my index finger, began tickling the sole.

"What?" squealed the ten-year-old. "Not fair! Stoppit!"

To give Herod his due, he held on for a few seconds before wriggling off Bella's back and out of range. He was on his feet with tears of anger in his eyes.

"What kind of fighting is that? That's baby fighting."

He was right, of course. But I was a thinker, not a fighter.

I stood up, coughing. "Listen, Herod. I'm willing to look into this organizer thing, but you have to let me follow proper procedure."

I picked up Herod's boot, holding it out, mainly to show everyone that I wasn't trying to steal it.

Things could have calmed down then. A lot of kids were drifting away for line-up. Bella was up but winded, and Herod was having a teary moment. The whole thing was running out of steam, and would probably have turned into a Hold-Me-Back, if Red Sharkey hadn't arrived.

Red burst into the center of the circle on a mountain bike, scattering bystanders like skittles. Red Sharkey had always been at the center of the rowdy crowd. Red made his points with fists and jibes. He was tall and wiry, with flaming red hair that had earned him his school-yard name. Most of the children and staff at Saint Jerome's didn't know Red's real name, and wouldn't use it if they did. Red was the oldest kid in middle school. He should have moved on to high school a year ago, but he hadn't attended much early on and had been held back.

For a moment, Red's eyes were wide and worried, then he saw his brother upright and apparently not bleeding. He jumped off his bike, kicking the stand with his heel during the dismount. I couldn't pull off a move like that if I practiced for a year.

"Roddy?" he said, with a casual nod.

Herod scowled at his brother. "I don't need you, Goody Two-shoes. I can handle this."

"So I see. Can't you stay out of trouble for a minute?"

Bella caught her breath. "Your brother stole my organizer. Brand new."

"I did not!" objected Herod.

Red frowned. "Whenever anything goes missing in this school, the nearest Sharkey gets the blame." He glanced at his brother. "You didn't take it, did you?"

"No."

"Are you sure?"

Herod took a second to think back over the past few days.

"Yeah. Certain. No organizer."

"Right, that's it. He didn't take it. End of story. Nothing to see here, let's move it along."

Good idea, I thought. Red has more sense than his brother.

But Bella wasn't backing down for anyone, even Red Sharkey.

"*He's* going to prove Herod did it."

Oh no, I thought. I'm *he*. *He's* me.

"Who's going to prove Herod did it?" demanded Red.

"He is!" shouted several dozen people. Most of them pointed, too.

Red turned, following the fingers. His accusing gaze settled on me.

"Hey, Red," I said, trying the friendly approach. "How you doing?"

Red smiled mirthlessly. "Half Moon. The man with the badge. This is not lost cats, this is the actual world. People could get in trouble."

I shrugged. "Tell your brother. He invited me."

"Doobie is always going on about his partner, the qualified detective, with the actual detective's badge," said Herod. "So let the nerd prove I'm innocent."

I didn't know which disturbed me more: Doobie calling me his partner or Herod calling me a nerd.

"Yeah, let the nerd prove he's innocent," said Bella, rubbing her neck. "Or else Herod's guilty, as far as I'm concerned."

Red rubbed his temples as though the stupidity of what he was hearing was giving him a headache. "Listen to me. Half Moon plays at being a detective. His mom bought him a toy badge somewhere, so now he goes around pretending to be Sherlock Holmes. It's not real. He can't *prove* anything."

This was too much. I imagined the badge in my pocket glowing with indignation. I took out the wallet, flipping it open..

"Actually, Red," I said. "This is a real detective's badge. I am a real detective. First in the academy."

Red turned slowly toward me. Generally, at this point, I would run away and find a dark corner to hide in, but some things are worth standing up for.

"So, you're a real detective. I bet criminals all over Ireland are turning themselves in. 'What's the point?' they're saying. 'Fletcher Moon is on the case.'"

"Go, Fletcher!" snuffled Doobie, who was too young for sarcasm.

"So what does your big detective's brain tell you about the case of the missing organizer?" continued Red.

I shrugged. "Nothing. I don't know the facts. I haven't had a chance to question anyone."

Red leaned back on the saddle of his bike. I got the feeling he was more interested in poking fun at me than clearing his brother's name. Although, in all fairness, it would take two dozen lawyers and a time machine to clear Herod's name completely.

"I'm sure Bella can answer any questions you care to ask," said Red, grinning in anticipation of my failure.

"Come on, Fletcher," said April Devereux. Her Barbie buddies did some cheerleading hops. It was nice to have somebody in my corner, even April and co. Although I suspected that they were more anti-Sharkey than pro-Moon.

I cleared my throat and tried to sound professional. "So, Miss . . . ah . . . Bella. Tell me what happened. Don't leave out any detail, however insignificant."

Bella thought for a moment. "Well, I got up at

seven, and I was thinking about these earrings for ages, 'cause Quinn says they're banned."

I interrupted her. "Okay. You can leave out those details, stuff that only happened in your head and not in the actual world. Just tell us about the organizer."

"Okay. It was a birthday present. Date book, phone numbers, MP3 player. Everything. If someone wanted to know the time in Tokyo, all they had to do was ask."

The crowd oohed, impressed. Bella accepted their admiration with a little royal wave.

"So I brought it in today for the first time. Only, I forgot about it for a minute 'cause I was worrying about the earrings. I left my bag by the wall and went off for a walk with the girls."

Bella and her friends spent a large part of their break time walking around. They would circle the yard, searching for little kids with no fashion sense to tease.

"So, halfway around, I remembered my organizer and ran back to my bag. But I was too late, little Klepto Sharkey had already made off with it."

"Klepto?" said Red, trying to sound incredulous.

"Yes, Red. Klepto. Short for kleptomaniac. He's a real Sharkey, all right. Been stealing since he was in diapers."

Red's expression was more resigned than furious.

"So maybe Roddy's been in trouble a few times, that's not proof of anything."

April Devereux took a step forward from the rank of pink go-gos.

"I saw him searching Bella's bag. I saw him with my actual vision. That's proof, isn't it? I watch *Law and Order*, so I know. I'm a witness."

I winced apologetically at Red. "That's pretty strong. An eyewitness."

"So where's the organizer?" countered Red. "If he stole it a few minutes ago, where is it?"

I transferred my wince to Bella. "That's pretty strong. No smoking gun."

"I know that, Half Moon. That's why you're here. You don't think I'd even be talking to you if I didn't need something."

All eyes were on me again, and not in a nice *Oh, look at that handsome young man in the shiny shoes, I wonder if he's single* kind of way. It was more of a nasty *If he doesn't come up with the goods in ten seconds, let's lynch him* kind of way.

I considered the facts aloud. "So, the organizer is missing, and Herod Sharkey is the prime suspect. But if Herod did steal it, then he obviously stashed it somewhere."

"Herod has little hidey-holes all over town," said April. "He's like some kind of rabbit, only one that steals stuff."

"This hidey-hole would have to be on the school grounds. He only had a minute before Bella confronted him. Where could he go in a minute?"

This was a question with as many answers as there were degrees on the compass. And with so many thousands of footprints tracking across the basketball court, it was impossible to isolate just one set. Unless Herod had brought something back from wherever it was he'd gone.

I still had Herod's hiking boot in my hand. I flicked it over and studied the deep sole, hoping for a clue. I found one. The rubber was stained yellow and there were several buttercups trapped in the ridges. They were freshly ripped from the soil, with barely a trace of brown on the petals.

"The Millennium Garden," I said, looking Herod straight in the face. He was suddenly pale and open-mouthed. A reaction that told me I was right, so I took off striding toward the school garden, leaving the rest to follow.

Those few moments, during the short walk from the basketball court to the garden, were the happiest moments I was to have for some time. This was what detective work was all about. Those precious seconds when you have made a breakthrough and you are so sure of it, that the confidence seems to burst through your very pores.

The buttercups trapped in Herod's boot told me exactly where he had been in the past few minutes. Several years ago, at the beginning of the new millennium, the school got a grant for a commemorative wild garden. Every spring we were treated to the story at assembly by Principal Quinn. The garden was designed in a ring pattern. One ring for each millennium, each ring a different color. Green, white, and gold like the Irish flag. Green grass, white daisies, and golden buttercups. Buttercups that were flowering again because of the Indian summer.

Of course it could mean nothing. Maybe Herod had just walked through the garden on his way to school, but his reaction made me think differently.

I arrived at the garden, dragging the rest behind me like the Pied Piper. I looked hard at the ground for several moments, then glanced sharply at Herod. He was staring at his own feet, but every few seconds his eyeballs would flick across to the buttercup ring. It was just as Bernstein said in chapter eight of the detective's manual. *The criminal's own body will betray him. Guilt is a powerful force and will find a way out.* In this case, through the eyes.

I stepped into the buttercup ring, careful to avoid crushing too many of Mrs. Quinn's precious flowers, and thrust my fingers into the loose clay in the center. Barely a centimeter down, I hit metal. There was a box down there.

"I have never seen that cookie tin before in my life," said Herod, jumping the gun a bit.

Red groaned. "Moron. How do you know it's a cookie tin?"

"I know," replied Herod haughtily, "because I

put it . . ." He stopped then, because the penny had dropped.

"Exactly," sighed Red. "As I said. Moron."

I was about to pull out the box when Bella barged me aside. She ripped the tin from the earth. Surprise, surprise, it was a cookie tin.

Bella flipped the lid and selected her organizer from the contents.

"Half Moon was right," she crowed. "You did take it, you little Sharkey thief. Now I am legally entitled to beat you the length of the school yard."

"That probably won't hold up in court," I said, from the ring of daisies.

Bella was not the only person annoyed with Herod. Red was having trouble containing himself.

"You promised me," he said, fists clenched in exasperation. "No more stealing in school. Don't you know what could happen to the family?"

"I didn't take it," protested Herod. "The box is mine, but I didn't put the organizer in it. This is a setup."

No one was convinced by this. Legend had it that Herod's first words were *I've been framed*.

I picked myself up from the ring, then leaned over, shaking flowers from my hair.

"In Herod's defense, this is far from conclusive," I said to my shoes. "There are missing links in the chain of evidence."

An impressed silence followed this technical-sounding statement; or so I thought. I looked up to find that it was more of a deserted silence. Everyone who had followed me to the Millennium Garden was now hightailing it back to the basketball courts. They moved with a speed and silence that would have shamed a special forces squad. Even Red Sharkey was moving quickly, although he managed to do it in a nonchalant way.

There was only one person in this school that could make Red Sharkey run anywhere. That person must be nearby, so I started to get a move on, too.

"Fletcher Moon. I don't believe it."

It was Principal Quinn. As usual she was flanked by Larry and Adam. I know dogs aren't supposed to smile, but I swear I could see them grinning behind their muzzles.

"Please tell me what you think you are doing."

Apparently, telling a teacher what you think you are doing makes you think about what you have done.

"I think I am going straight down to the office," I answered, hoping a bit of humor would lighten the tension.

Mrs. Quinn chuckled, and for a second I was hopeful; then her laughter dried up like a water hole in the Sahara.

"Correct," she snapped. "When I get back from line-up inspection, you had better be there waiting."

It seemed to me that Larry and Adam sniggered then, or perhaps they growled. I didn't know which was worse. Mrs. Quinn led them off to make sure that the class lines were as straight as rulers.

I trudged back through the school field toward the main building. The euphoria I had felt earlier drained down through the soles of my feet. Yes, I had solved the case, but I had broken Bernstein's first rule: *Never become a piece of the puzzle*. A detective should not be afraid of the outcome of a case, as this fear will affect his work. The victim, witness, and perpetrator had all known where to find me if my findings went against them. The Sharkeys had tried to use me, but it had backfired on them, and now Herod was a marked man. I was a marked man too, or I would be. Several marks probably, if Red had his way.

The school "bell" rang. It was a computer bell that used a sample of Mrs. Quinn's own voice. "Line up, students," the bell said. "Don't make me ask again." Of course it did ask again. Over and over again. Jimín Grady had been expelled recently for sneaking into the office and replacing Mrs. Quinn's voice sample with his own. His message had not been quite so polite.

I was just picking up my bag, when Red Sharkey appeared from inside the porch shadows. He emerged from the darkness one limb at a time, like a cartoon villain.

"You think you're very smart, don't you, Half Moon?" he said, his eyes blazing with unpredictable anger.

"My name is Fletcher," I said, feeling pretty proud of myself for not allowing my shaking knees to fold underneath me.

"Well, *Fletcher*, I better not hear any more about this organizer thing. I have enough trouble without a toy detective stirring things up."

There was something new in Red's voice as he said this. The anger was still in there, but there was desperation, too. And I got the feeling that the anger was not all directed at me.

"As far as I'm concerned it's a closed case, but I'd advise your brother to steer clear of Bella for a while."

Red nodded, accepting the advice, then remembered that he was supposed to be angry at me. He leaned in close, brushing against me.

"Roddy will steer clear of Bella, and you steer clear of us. As of now, Half Moon, you are retired. Got it?"

I stared him down. I wasn't retiring for him or anyone else. I thought I was being really brave holding his gaze like that, but five minutes later I realized that this was just what Red Sharkey wanted. It gave him the opportunity to steal my badge.

I GET A STICK FIGURE

I SAT ON ONE OF THE baby seats outside Mrs. Quinn's door waiting for the red light to turn green. Red meant Do not disturb; green meant Knock. This was a code that even the kindergartners could follow.

I felt sick to my stomach. My badge was gone. Just like that, I was back to being a normal kid. Of course, I knew in theory that the badge was just a hunk of metal, and that I was just as much a detective without it. But I had studied for two years to win that badge, and for the past six months it had made me feel special, extraordinary. Without it, I was just another kid who thought he was Sherlock Holmes.

I had to get my badge back, that's all there was to it. I knew where it was, or rather I knew who knew where it was, but I had zero evidence and even less chance of a confession. But where there was a theft, there was evidence. I would find that evidence and present it to Red. Then he could either give me back my shield, or I would take my evidence to the police.

Someone sat beside me. I was amazed to find it was April Devereux. She grinned, and I could see a lump of neon-blue chewing gum behind her perfect teeth.

"Hi, April. Are you in trouble, too?"

April shook her head, setting rows of pink beads in her hair rattling like snakes. "Hardly. I don't do trouble. Just delivering a *message* for Fitz." April pronounced *message* the French way.

Mr. Fitzgerald was our teacher. He thought allowing us to call him *Fitz* would make him cool and trendy. He had about as much chance of being cool as I had of winning Olympic gold in the high jump.

"I just stopped to ask how much you charge?"

"Charge?"

April pulled a ten-euro note from her pocket.

"For detective work. Like finding the organizer."

"I suppose ten would be fair for today. I did put myself at considerable risk."

April laughed. "Are you serious, Half Moon? I didn't hire you for that. You were soooo lucky with that cookie tin, by the way. A pedicure is thirty, so you'd be, like, a third that important. So I'll give you this ten for a retainer. If you take it, then you work for me."

I didn't ignore the note, but I didn't grab it either. I wasn't really used to dealing with girls, unless I was questioning them about missing pencil cases or asking some of the rougher ones to give me back my lunch box.

"A retainer? To investigate what?"

April stood, flicking her hair over one shoulder. With her pink puff jacket on, she looked like a marshmallow.

"It's more Sharkey trouble, I'm afraid. Not just the little stinky one. The whole family."

I patted the pocket where my badge used to be. Red Sharkey was involved. I had already decided to investigate the Sharkeys, this could be a way to make a few euros while I was about it. Do a bit of snooping around for April, and dig up some dirt on Red. Who knows, I may even catch him red-handed with my badge. A couple of surveillance photos later, and the long arm of the law would be getting a lot shorter for Red.

"Okay," I said. "Tell me all about this case."

April had pulled out a compact mirror, and was checking her reflection.

"*Bonjour,*" she said to herself in the mirror. "How are you? You look great. Have you lost weight?"

I cleared my throat. "Hello. April. The case?"

April snapped the mirror closed.

"Sorry, Half Moon. I was just taking a moment to boost my self-esteem. I saw that on the mental health channel. The case. Well, I thought it was crazy at first, but there is definitely something strange going on in Lock."

Suddenly the door light flashed green.

"Enter!" shrilled the principal's voice through the door.

"I'd better go in," I said, struggling out of the baby chair.

April caught my sleeve. "Come around to my house. After dinner."

Another shout from inside. Louder this time.

"I'll be there," I said, reaching for the door handle. "About seven."

"'Kay," said April. "But don't spread it around. We're not, like, on the same level. I don't want people to think we're having a rendezvous or anything. You work for me, like a maid or something. A nerdy maid."

I kept a straight face. Enduring disrespect was a detective's lot. Still, April was exceptionally obnoxious. I was used to insults from my own age group, but April was only ten, and at least four inches shorter than me. And if you're four inches shorter than me, then you're short.

See you then, I thought, and entered the principal's office smiling grimly. The badge would be mine again, even if I had to suffer April Devereux to get it.

* * *

Mrs. Quinn was moored behind an undersized desk from one of the elementary classrooms. The desk was swamped with report cards and official forms, and somewhere beneath the cables of her knitted cardigan, a phone rang. The principal ignored it.

The two Dobermans, Larry and Adam, stood at the principal's shoulders. Without their muzzles on, it was clear that they actually *were* grinning.

I remembered why I was there and stopped smiling.

"Well, little Fletcher Moon," said Mrs. Quinn delightedly. "What a nice surprise." Then *she* remembered why I was there, and her expression turned hard. The dogs stopped smiling, too. Spittle hung in strings from their jaws.

Principals are able to switch moods in seconds. They would make excellent schizophrenics. "Do you have anything to say for yourself? Any extenuating circumstances, perhaps?"

I shook my head; getting someone else involved would be social suicide. "No. I just forgot where I was walking."

Mrs. Quinn pointed to a small molded plastic chair in front of her desk. "Every day we lose another one. Sit."

I sat. Another baby chair. My knees collided with my chin, clicking my teeth together.

Mrs. Quinn pulled a huge book from a drawer. It was covered with patterned velvet wallpaper.

"I'm going to show you something, Fletcher. This is my personal ledger. In this book I keep a record of every single child that ever passed through Saint Jerome's."

The book looked about a hundred years old. I half expected dragons to fly out when she opened it. Each page was divided into rows, one per child. After each child's name was a series of boxes, with a picture drawn in every one.

"This is my own method of recording. It's easy to review at a glance. I'm afraid you'll be getting a general rowdiness picture today." She hauled several yellowed pages across, until she arrived at the current students.

"Here we go. A fine crop of future world leaders."

I suspected Mrs. Quinn was being sarcastic, but I couldn't be sure. Maybe she had more faith in us than we had in ourselves.

"Look here. Lovely little May Devereux in fifth grade. Never caused a day's trouble in her life."

May was April's first cousin. Their fathers were brothers and joined at the hip, and so were their daughters whether they liked it or not. They were even connected by the *months of the year* names, which their parents thought were impossibly cute. The school yard grapevine had it that April was embarrassed that May wasn't quite as *pink* as she should be.

"Look at May's pictures. An abacus, because she's

such a good little math scholar. A pair of dancing shoes, because she danced in last year's talent show. And an angel, because that's what she is. Not many people have pictures like May Devereux."

I was starting to get the picture. Pardon the pun.

"Oh, I see," I said, pointing to another row of pictures. "There's Dermot Carmody. There's a picture of him sitting by the fire, because he got a summer job in Riley's Bakery."

Mrs. Quinn sighed, disappointed. "No, Fletcher. Wake up, boy. Those are the flames of hell. Dermot dropped out of school, so that's where he's headed. See the little horns?"

"Aah," I said, holding on to the chair in case my legs decided to get up and run away.

Mrs. Quinn pointed to another row of tiny pictures. "Here's Red Sharkey. You see what his first picture is?"

I leaned in to see. In the box was a crude drawing of an agitated stick figure. "General rowdiness," I guessed.

"Well done, Fletcher. Top of the class. General rowdiness. That's how it always starts. A harmless bit of playacting. But before you know it, you're on to the serious stuff, just like Red. Fighting, cutting class, suspension."

There was a picture for each crime. Suspension was wittily displayed by a lynched stickfigure.

"And now, on to Fletcher Moon. What do we

32

have here? Only good things. Look, a little bee. . . ."

"I won the spelling bee in first grade."

Mrs. Quinn punched me playfully on the shoulder. I almost fell out of the baby chair.

"Now you're getting it, Fletcher. Who says you're thick? And next we have a little magnifying glass. Because?"

Another easy one. "Because I was forced to . . . Because I volunteered to find your keys last year."

Mrs. Quinn dealt me another jokey blow. I felt my arm go numb. The principal selected a chubby stump crayon from the pack and drew a general rowdiness stick figure in my third box.

"Now, Fletcher," she said sadly. "You are branded forever. Let's hope that this is as far as it goes. I wouldn't like to see you following the same pattern as Red."

"No, ma'am."

"We don't want you ending up with the flames of hell, or in a little *nee-naa*."

"Police car?"

"Exactly. It's really quite a scientific system. I can read trends and predict behavior. Sometimes I punish people in advance, because my little boxes tell me what they're going to do."

I felt it was time for a speech. "Don't worry about Fletcher Moon, ma'am. I've learned my lesson. No more stick figures for me."

Mrs. Quinn shut the ledger with a thump. "I

hope not. Now off you go. You didn't see who was next, did you? I do hope it's a naughty child so I can really enjoy administering the punishment. I couldn't bear another fallen angel."

The feeling was returning to my arm. That feeling was pain.

"I was the only one, unless someone arrived while I've been in here."

"Only one way to find out," said Mrs. Quinn, bright-eyed. She flicked the door light from red to green.

As the door closed behind me, I didn't know who to be sorry for, Mrs. Quinn or whoever was next in to see her. In the hallway, a kindergartner with tousled hair and a bloody nose was sucking his thumb.

"Enter!" howled the principal at the top of her lungs. Larry and Adam took up the howl until it echoed down the hall.

I'M ON THE CASE

MY MOTHER WORRIES about me. She worries that I'm not going to grow, or that I'm going to hit a spurt and cost her a fortune in new clothes. She worries that I don't have many friends, and she worries about my fascination with crime.

I try to smile when she's around to show how happy I am, but I'm not really a smiler so she knows I'm faking. So then I don't smile and she follows me around asking what's wrong.

That day, when she came to my room to check homework, for once I was able to tell her something that made her happy.

"I'm going over to April Devereux's house after dinner."

Mom was ecstatic. "Oh my God. April Devereux. April and May are the cutest names. It takes a lot of guts, as a parent, to give your children names like that, but if they turn out pretty then it's worth the risk. What are you going to say?"

"Nothing. I'm going to listen. April wants to talk to me."

Mom waved her hands in the air in thanks. "April Devereux wants to talk to my little Fletcher. She's so pretty. Perfect. You have to say something, honey. You can't sit there nodding for the evening."

I was beginning to wish I hadn't mentioned my appointment.

"I will respond to the situation, Mom. Whatever comes up."

Mom drew a horrified breath. "Oh, no you don't. I know how you respond to situations, Fletcher Moon. You make one of your observational deductions. You told your cousin Eve that she had a calcium deficiency."

"She did. There were white spots on her nails. I was just trying to help."

Mom shook me by the shoulders, then squeezed me tight. "Trust me, honey. That isn't what girls want to hear. Just tell us we look fabulous as often as possible."

I frowned. "Even if it's not true?"

Mom pulled three of my shirts from the closet. "Especially if it's not true. Now, which one?"

I pointed to a plain black shirt, which I would wear with plain black jeans. Be invisible.

"Mom, you should maybe calm down a little. It's not a social call. April wants my help. She's a client. And she's only ten."

Mom rolled her eyes. "Men. Such simpletons. Honestly. Do you think I told your father that I thought he was handsome? No. I told him I needed his help with physics."

"And Dad fell for that?"

"Of course he did. He wanted to fall for it, and I didn't even take physics."

Mom was an interior decorator who ran her own business from the garage. Dad was a computer engineer with a local company that made memory boards. They were an unlikely match. Art and science. Heart and hand.

My sister, Hazel, stomped into my room, not bothering to knock. She was fifteen, an aspiring writer, and a full-time drama queen. Hazel could be found at any given hour either hunched over her antique typewriter or fending off the droves of adolescent boys that she attracts with her fine features and blond hair. Fending off all except her beloved Stevie.

Hazel took a sheet of paper from her bag.

"I need your professional opinion, Fletcher," she said, handing me the folded note. Hazel was perhaps the only person in the world who took my profession seriously. Except perhaps April Devereux, now.

I unfolded the paper and read a note from Hazel's boyfriend.

Dear Hazel,

 I am so sorry about the movies last night. Dad made me stay in and write my history assignment about the Battle of the Somme in World War II.

 I will make it up to you. Next weekend let me take you for dinner at Le Bistro. My treat.

       XXXXX
       Stevie

I rubbed the page between my fingers, then smelled it.

"Well?" demanded Hazel. "What do you think?"

I scratched my chin. "I would have to say, dump him."

Hazel stamped her foot. "I knew it!" she whined. "How do you know?"

"There are several clues. First he blames his father, which is classic transference. Then he refers to the Battle of the Somme, which took place in World War One, not Two—something Stevie would know if he had actually completed his assignment. Also specific references such as the essay title are commonly woven into false stories to make them sound real. In fact they provide the detective with more ways to trip up the subject."

"This is all pretty circumstantial."

I took a pot of graphite filings from my desk. "I'm not finished yet," I said. "Stevie offers to bring you to Le Bistro, which is gross overcompensation. That has guilt written all over it. The letter smells faintly of perfume, Happy by Clinique, which is not one of yours, which leads me to believe he has been holding hands with another girl. Finally, I feel indentations in the page. I suspect that our Stevie made more than one attempt to write this letter. Perhaps he was even going to tell the truth before he lost his nerve."

I laid the page flat on my desk, shaking graphite filings over its surface. After a slow count of ten, I tipped the filings into the wastepaper basket. Not all the filings ran off, some caught in the indents.

"This is what was written on the page before this one in the pad. Only two lines are legible. I think you will find that the handwriting is the same."

Hazel took the sheet, reading the faint black writing aloud. *"Dear Hazel, I don't know how to tell you this, but I have met some . . ."* My sister ripped the note into shreds, tossing it into the air like confetti.

"He's met someone else, has he?" she said, pulling a cell phone out of her pocket. "Someone who wears Happy. It should take me about five minutes to find out who." She handed me a Mars bar. "Thanks, little brother. For that I won't tease you for an entire day."

"I'd prefer actual money," I said.

"I can't pay you," said Hazel, skipping across the

hall to her own room. "It would be exploitation of child labor."

The door closed behind her.

Mom sighed. "We won't see her for days. Hazel will get at least a one-act play out of this."

I knelt to gather the shreds of paper. "Do you see how complicated things become when people get involved in relationships, Mom? My business is just taking off and I want to concentrate on that, so I think I'll give the relationships a pass for a few years, if you don't mind. April Devereux is a client, that's all."

"Okay," said Mom. "But wear something with color. Think ahead. You never know."

How do you know if you're a detective? What sets us apart from the everyday people? My theory is that most people like to dwell on the brighter side of life. They want to concentrate on the rug, and not on the dirt swept underneath. Not detectives. We want to pull back the rug and put the dirt in a forensics bag. Then we want to run over the floorboards with a sticky roller just in case some of the dirt got away. We are social scientists. We like to take people apart to see what makes them tick. You don't have to be particularly smart to be a detective, you just have to want to do it.

April lived on Rhododendron Road. A name that must have started out as a joke and then stuck. It took twenty-five minutes to walk along Lock's historic wooden works and across the town bridge, and with every step I thought about my badge.

April's house was a large manor-style building, complete with manicured lawns and a tree-lined avenue. The drive was covered with raked white gravel, and flower beds swirled along both sides drawing the visitor toward the front porch.

I crunched down the drive only to be told by the gardener that April was next door at her cousin's, but had left a note for me. The note was on scented pink paper with a unicorn watermark. April Devereux was printed in dark-pink flowing script across the top.

> Dear Half Moon,
> Follow the yellow brick road.
> A (April)

It was not very encouraging, I decided, if your employer thought you were too thick to figure out that A stood for April. Especially at the bottom of a note from April, on April's personally monogrammed paper.

The yellow brick road was a sandstone path that wound through the white gravel, leading to a gate in the wall between April's and May's houses. The gate was unlocked and I pushed through to a house pretty much identical to the first one.

April's cousin May ran down her side of the yellow brick road, just as I closed the gate.

"Fletcher," she said. "You came. I was just coming to check."

It was generally acknowledged that May Devereux was the nice one of the pair. She was dressed in full Irish dance costume, including hard shoes. Gold and green were the prominent colors. This, I have to admit, was a surprise.

"Practicing?"

She grimaced. "Yes. I want to do better this year in the school talent show. Only a few days to go."

"I'm sure you will," I said kindly. May's chances of doing well in any show were about as promising as mine of going on a dream date with Bella Barnes. It was well known in our class that May was the worst dancer in this universe and perhaps any parallel ones. When May tapped out a hornpipe on a wooden floor, it was like listening to a toddler trying to crush a spider with a hammer.

"Nice costume," I said.

"It's my lucky dress," said May. "Nice shirt."

Mom wouldn't let me out of the house dressed completely in black; she felt I would be broadcasting negative vibrations. So I agreed to wear a Hawaiian shirt given to me by an uncle who didn't really know me as a person.

I shrugged apologetically. "My mother . . ."

May nodded. No further explanation was needed. Everyone in Lock knew about my mother's flamboyant taste in color.

May's father appeared behind her, in full gardening regalia, including leather kneepads and thorn-proof gloves. He was tall and lean with a farmer's tan. In fact, he looked exactly how TV said a father should look, right down to the checkered sweater. He seemed the perfect dad and husband. My mother and her art appreciation group had been genuinely shocked when May's mother had walked out on the family a few months earlier.

"Mr. Devereux," I said, extending a hand. "I'm Fletcher Moon."

May's father shook the hand, smiling. Perfect white teeth, of course.

"Call me Gregor. Ah, yes, the young detective. May tells me you have qualifications."

"That's right. I'm certified to practice in the U.S. Washington, to be precise, when I'm twenty-one."

Mr. Devereux nodded seriously. "That's very impressive, Fletcher. Maybe you can help April and May solve this crime of theirs. Or you could, if the girls weren't completely loopy and imagining the whole thing."

May's father winked at me, rotating his index finger by his temple. International sign language for completely loopy.

"Dad," said May, elbowing her father in the ribs.

Mr. Devereux groaned theatrically, clutching his side. "Okay, okay. There *is* a big conspiracy. Everyone *else* is loopy, except the two cute cousins."

May grabbed my hand. "Come on. April is in the Wendy house."

I was happy to find myself dragged through a garden by a pretty girl from the pink set, but I wasn't quite as enthusiastic about sitting in a Wendy house. That's the kind of thing that can get you killed if it leaks out to the boys in school. We followed the path past a seashell fountain complete with frolicking cherubs, which looked like it hadn't worked in decades. But this Wendy house was no plastic hut crammed with dollies and toy tea sets. This was an actual mini-house with electricity, Internet access, and running water.

When we entered, April was at a laptop, poring over a world economics Web page. It was a nice system, linked up to a scanner, printer, and digital camera.

"Fletcher's here," said May.

April started, then shook a tiny fist at the computer. "Just a sec. I'm trying to check out the latest red carpet gossip, and this educational junk keeps popping up. Honestly, market strengths in Asia. Like, who cares?"

"A few billion Asians," I said.

April scowled at me. I was starting to feel very unloved. That didn't bother me much. Detectives had to get used to negativity. One of our main functions is to bring bad news.

April shut the computer's lid and faced me. If she had been pink in school, now she had gone into pink overdrive. She was wearing so much pink that it cast a glow onto the walls.

"Pink!" I blurted.

I was treated to a twirl. "I know. Isn't it fabulous? Us girls love pink. It's the essence of femininity."

I was starting to feel that at least some of this pinkness was for my benefit.

May took two bottles of chilled water from the fridge, handing one to me.

"Nice place," I said.

"Dad built it for me so that I can practice my dancing. He really wants me to win a medal or something."

"I'm sure you will. Someday."

How could I say that? What a phony.

April changed the subject. "We should talk about my case. How much of your valuable time do those ten euros buy?"

This was it. The big time. "I charge a fee of ten euros per day. Plus expenses. But because this is my first real case, I'm going to waive the expenses. And because of school and homework, it generally takes me about three days to put in a full day's work. So I'm all yours until Sunday."

April took out her wallet and peeled ten euros from a roll. If she became a regular customer, my rates would have to go up.

"Now I own you for a week."

I had to think about this for a moment. April was

not the noble kind of client I had always imagined. Her father was not a kidnapped professor, nor was she searching for a missing orphanage fund. But on the plus side, this case was about the Sharkeys, and she did have a big roll of cash.

I took the money and slipped it into my breast pocket. Now I could buy my own chocolate, instead of accepting it as payment. The money felt good in my pocket. It made me feel like a real private detective.

"Okay. That's the formalities out of the way, now what do you want investigated?"

April opened her mouth to answer, but May spoke first. "Are you sure, April? You know, Fletcher is not a bad person. He could get in trouble."

April glared at her. Her glare was so intense that you completely forgot she was wearing pink.

"Of course I'm sure, cousin. Why don't you go and do your Riverdance thing, and let me worry about Fletcher? He's supposed to be this great big detective."

"April is right," I said reassuringly to May. "Trouble goes with the badge."

April and May stared each other down for a long moment, like two Manga girls about to throw lightning bolts. For some reason, May didn't want me involved. Maybe she thought I was stupid, or maybe she was actually worried about me. Whatever the reason, I was more intrigued than ever.

Once their eyeballs dried up, April and May

called off the staring match and settled for not talking to each other. May continued to irritate April by taking off her hard shoes and drumming them on the desktop.

April waited for a break in the shoe tattoo before starting her story.

"The Sharkeys are major pains," she began. "They must have stolen a million things from people, which is totally illegal."

A million and one, I thought.

"I don't care about this usually," continued April. "'Cause it happens to other people who are not me. But a couple of weeks ago, the Sharkeys stole something from *moi*."

I pulled a small spiral notebook from my pocket. "How do you know it was the Sharkeys?"

April's eyes widened and I noticed she was wearing pink eye shadow. "'Cause I know, okay, Half Moon?"

I shook my head in a wise sort of way. "Just knowing isn't evidence, April."

April wasn't in the mood for wisdom. "I don't have video evidence or anything, but I just know. Plus, don't take that tone with me, like I'm a baby or something. You may be older than me, but I am cooler than you times infinity, so that cancels out the years."

I was about to argue further, then I remembered that I *just knew* Red had taken my badge.

"Okay. Tell me what happened."

"I bought a lock of Shona Biederbeck's hair on eBay."

I swallowed a smirk. Had April just used the words *bought* and *hair* in the same sentence?

"It's laminated and the plastic is autographed. It meant more to me than anything." April hugged an imaginary lock of hair to her heart.

I wrote down what she said, trying to be non-judgmental. I mean, who would actually pay money for some pop star's cast-off follicles?

"You think Red Sharkey stole this . . . ah . . . hair sample?"

"Definitely. He asked me for a look at it, begged me. And I told him sure, as soon as he could list the tracks on Shona's last CD in order, from memory. So he storms off, saying how he's gonna get a look at the hair one way or the other, and the next day it's one hundred percent gone."

The facts of the case lay before me, and I wasn't impressed. I was already feeling low over the theft of my badge, and now my big case turned out to be a missing curl. This was not a good career day for Fletcher Moon, ace detective. I closed my notebook.

"Listen, April. I think you better take your money back. I'm a detective. Missing hair isn't really my strong suit. Diamonds, relatives, even pets. But hair? I just can't. I'm trying to put together a reputation. It's just hair, and it's probably behind the sofa."

April was horrified. "Just hair!" she whispered. "That's like calling pink *just a color*. Are you insane, Half Moon? That curl from Shona Biederbeck's very own head is much more than just hair. It *was* the centerpiece on my project on culture. I had all these little photos and arrows pointing in at the curl. What are they going to point at now? A blank square? And for your information, Mr. Detective, behind the sofa was the first place I looked."

She had a point. But not one I particularly cared about. This must have shown in my face, because April gave me a look so piercing it could have bored holes in sheet steel.

"Red and Herod control our school like some kind of mini-Mafia, running around stealing whatever they want. Then they bring it home to their pig of a father, and he fences it, or whatever the word is. Here *you* are, a nerd calling himself a detective, too grand to take the case."

"Red's not so bad," said May, in a quiet voice. "He's never been caught stealing."

"He's never been *caught*," agreed April, then looked pointedly at me. "Until now, right, Fletcher?"

April made a strong case. I wasn't just looking for a lock of pop star hair. I was trying to bring down an entire crime family. The Sharkeys had made one enemy too many when they stole from April Devereux. And of course, I was pretty certain that Red had stolen my badge.

I reopened my notebook. "Okay. I'm hired. Tell me what happened."

April's mood instantly lifted. She was once again all white teeth and pink eye shadow.

"We keep all our cool stuff right here in the Wendy house. The morning after I brought the Shona curl to school, someone took it from my love heart strongbox."

"Could Red have known where the hair was?"

April frowned for a second. "All the girls knew. It would've been easy for him to find out. You know Red, always sweet-talking the ladies."

"Wasn't the Wendy house locked?"

"Yes. But we keep a spare key under the unicorn statue. The unicorn is my personal symbol, by the way. Maybe Red found it and put it back afterward."

There wasn't much to go on. No evidence, not even circumstantial. Just a couple of hunches, and as Bernstein said: *No one was ever convicted on a hunch.*

"Here's what I am going to do. First, I need to dig into the Sharkey family history. I also need to initiate surveillance, concentrating on Red as the main suspect. If we can catch him in some criminal act, then perhaps we can pressure him into returning your keepsake and the . . ."

I stopped short, unwilling to tell April about my badge. I was embarrassed about the incident; but also knowledge was power, and the more I talked to April the less I wanted her having any power over me.

May looked sharply at me.

"Returning the what?"

"All the other stuff he's taken," I said. "Some of it, at any rate."

April was too excited to pick up on my near-mistake.

"God, Fletcher, this is a totally new you. It's like you know what to do or something. It's really *CSI*."

CSI? I wished. All I had was a notebook and some brains. Not an electron microscope in sight.

"Shouldn't you dust for fingerprints?"

"I could do that," I said gently, eager to avoid sarcasm with a paying client. "But then I'd have to print everyone who's ever been in here, and even if I did that, those prints would be useless unless we actually found the laminated curl, by which time we'd probably already know who took it."

April sighed. "The police wouldn't dust for fingerprints either; they wouldn't even come to the house."

"The police are busy with stuff like bank robberies and fugitive hunts. Missing hair cases are best left to a private detective."

"Like you."

I snapped my notebook shut. "Exactly."

If you're outside the system, then you need a contact on the inside. I had a special relationship with a police officer in Lock going back over three years. So far all the information had been going one way, from me to him. Now it was finally time to reverse the flow of traffic.

I phoned him from the pay phone outside the station on my way home that evening. We met on a park bench fifteen minutes later.

"Nice shirt, Fletcher," said Sergeant Murt Hourihan. "You looking for a job in a surf store?"

Being a law enforcement agent, Murt felt he had to begin every conversation with a smart comment.

Hourihan laughed at his own joke, then got down to business.

"What do you have for me, Fletcher?"

The sergeant hid behind his newspaper as he spoke, as though we weren't talking. Just two people who happened to be sharing a bench. Murt did this for my benefit. He thought we were playing a little game.

"I charted all those auto thefts from that case."

"I tried that, Fletcher. What do you think, you're the only one with a brain around here? There was no *obvious* pattern."

I pulled a printout from my jeans pocket. "There is a pattern. Look."

I slid the printout along the bench. Sergeant Hourihan picked it up, unfolding it behind his newspaper. A smile spread across his face.

"There are two groups of thieves," he said finally.

"That's right. When you realize that, then there

are two clear centers of activity. If I were you, I'd look for chop shops near the old bridge and south of the Red Hen Tavern. Watch out for teenagers in BMWs."

Hourihan pocketed the page. "I already did. We have a car at both locations."

I was surprised. "I'm surprised. Is this some kind of test?"

Murt folded the printout, sliding it into his jacket pocket. "I'm just helping you to be all you can be. It's a valuable lesson. Sometimes when you can't find a pattern it's because there is more than one. Nice work, Moon. See you next week."

"Wait, Sergeant. I need a favor."

Hourihan's smile widened. "What? Do you need more chocolate already?"

This chocolate thing was getting out of hand. I was acquiring a reputation. "No. I've got chocolate all wrapped up. I want information."

"Information? You sound like a real detective, Fletcher."

Of course I was a real detective.

"I need to see anything you have on the Sharkeys."

Murt folded the paper. "The Sharkeys? Papa Sharkey and co. Those Sharkeys?"

"Those are the ones. I'm following a few leads."

Murt rolled his paper into a tube and pointed it at me like a baton.

"Now listen here, Fletcher. I'm all for you having a look at old cases, even letting you have a look at the odd Investigations map. I enjoy our little chats. But the Sharkeys? That's different. Papa isn't the sort of person you want to get involved with. He's smart, too. Never done a day in prison, unlike most of his relatives. No, you stay well away from the Sharkeys. The last thing you want to do is become a blip on Papa's radar. If he finds out who you are, or worse still, where you live, then life could become very uncomfortable for you." Murt gave me a stern stare, perfected by years of interrogating suspects. "Do I make myself clear, Moon?"

Murt had given me the stare before, so I wasn't too intimidated.

"What if you gave me a look at the Sharkey file, and if I figure anything out I tell you straight away?"

Murt chortled. "God, you're a chancer, Fletcher. You have more neck than a herd of giraffes. First of all, you wouldn't be able to carry the Sharkey file it's so thick, and secondly that file is very active. I'd have to get a written presidential order before I could let you look at an active file. I like you, Fletcher, but I'm not prepared to be stationed on some island off the west coast for you."

I sighed. "Okay, Sergeant. I'll forget about the Sharkeys."

Murt closed one eye, focusing the other on me. "You're not lying, are you, Fletcher? My policeman's eye always knows."

"No, Murt. I'm not lying."

Of course I was lying.

I ran home, and managed to make it into upstairs without the third degree from Mom and Dad. My sister, Hazel, was waiting on the landing chewing on a pencil.

"Fletcher, what's another word for rejected?"

I thought for a second. "Em . . . How about unwanted?"

Hazel jotted it down. "Good. And how about a rhyme for pathetic?"

That was a bit harder. "Ah . . . would prosthetic do?"

"I could work it in."

I paused by my door. "What are you working on, anyway? Something about you and Stevie?"

"No," said Hazel innocently. "An epic poem about your date with April Devereux."

I scowled at her, but realized there was no percentage in answering back. God only knew how long Hazel had been waiting for me to come home. She would have all her bases covered.

Inside, I sat on my office chair, rolling over to the desk. A quick tap on the track pad woke up my iBook laptop. I stared at the FBI wallpaper on the screen and thought about what I intended to do.

If I planned to proceed with this case, I needed information, and the only way to get that information was to access the police Web site and download the Sharkey file. Did I want to break the case that much? Or was I just doing it for my badge?

A thought struck me. Maybe there was a way to get a new badge. I logged on to the Bernstein Web site and typed *replacement badge* into their search engine. The paragraph that popped up was not encouraging. Any requests for a replacement badge must be accompanied by two hundred dollars and a police report. Maybe I could scrape together the money after a year or so, but forging a police document was a serious crime.

I had only two choices: give up now, or hack the site. No need to choose just yet, I told myself. Maybe you won't be able to access the site, and the choice will be taken out of your hands.

I opened the police site's welcome page. I needed a name, rank, number, and password to proceed. I had three out of four. Name, rank, and number were easy. Password was a different matter, but I had a hunch.

Murt Hourihan had two passions. One was law enforcement, which he was much better at than he pretended. The second was greyhound racing. He loved the sport so much that he had joined a police syndicate to buy a dog. The dog's name was *Blue Flew*. I typed in the words.

The iBook clicked and whirred for a moment, then welcomed Sergeant Hourihan to the site. I was in.

The site was based on a common law-enforcement template used by police forces worldwide, and had several sections, including resources, keyword search, county by county, recent arrests, and incident reports.

I felt a slight thrill of guilt. What I was doing was not illegal as such—citizens were entitled to access to these files under the freedom of information act. But a minor certainly should not be trawling through active files without supervision.

I selected our county, then chose *Lock* from the drop-down menu. I narrowed the search further by typing the surname *Sharkey* in a flashing box. A colored circle whirled on the screen while the site compiled a list of Sharkey-related incidents. Eventually, a relevant list opened on a fresh page. There were over a hundred open cases with a Sharkey tag attached to them. This was incredible. Sergeant Hourihan had shown me closed case files before, and nobody had come near to a hundred tags. Even Dublin's notorious General was only associated with fifty unsolved cases.

I scanned the file headings briefly. Nearly all of the offenses were grand or petty larceny. It looked as though the Sharkeys were responsible for an ongoing crime wave in Lock that had lasted over ten years. Well, if I had anything to say about it, their crime wave was about to break.

My fingers hovered over apple+p. If I printed

these three hundred–plus pages, I was setting off on a road that might be difficult to exit. Was my badge really worth that much to me?

Yes, I decided. *It was.*

I pressed the keys.

CHAPTER

MAKING AN IMPRESSION—
ON MY FOREHEAD

I REMEMBER MY FIRST CASE. I was three years old, closed in a playpen in downtown Lock. One of the day care workers, Monique, took off her engagement ring while she was sterilizing bottles. She put the bottles in the microwave, and when she went back to the countertop, the ring was gone. It wasn't the kind of ring you could mislay, a big hunk of zircon. Someone had taken it. Monique was hysterical, tearing the place apart. It took three women to stop her from ripping out the plumbing.

I remember sitting on a beanbag, chewing on an animal cracker, thinking it over. I knew who had taken the ring. A toddler called Mary Ann who loved shiny things. I hadn't actually seen her take it, and I knew enough about playground law to know that you didn't shoot your mouth off without proof. I decided to get proof because Mary Ann had swiped one of my chocolate fingers the week before. She was a repeat offender and she had to be stopped.

I waddled over to the crime scene and had a good poke around. When I had everything I needed, I brought my case to the sobbing caregiver.

"Mary Ann took the ring," I told them.

Monique tried to be professional through her hysteria. "Now, Fletcher, we've talked about this. No making up stories."

"Mary Ann took the ring," I insisted, scowling through the cracker crumbs around my lips.

Mary Ann picked up a building block and hefted it at my head. It made solid contact, felling me like a tree trunk. Once the bleeding had stopped, I made a second attempt to break the case.

"Mary Ann took the ring," I said again. "Come see."

I dragged Monique over to the sink.

"Look," I said, pointing to a red smear on the stainless steel, near where the ring had been. "Jam. Mary Ann had jam."

Monique's expression changed from patient to interested.

"That's true, I suppose, but other people had jam."

I had more evidence. "Look. On the floor. Marks."

Monique checked the floor. Wet tracks led across the tiles and onto the Disney rug. Four tracks. A walker.

"Mary Ann has wheels," I said.

It was the clincher. Only Mary Ann had jam and a walker. She was quickly stripped and searched. They found the ring stuffed down her diaper along with three marbles, a plastic dinosaur, and two sets of car keys. I know now that Mary Ann was suffering from what detectives called Magpie Syndrome.

I thought that my cleverness would make me popular. I was wrong. No one wants a friend who can find out their secrets. Somehow I realized even at three years old that if I wanted friends, I would have to stop finding things out. I didn't stop, and Mary Ann has hated me now for almost a decade. If she wants to do anything about it after all this time, she'll just have to join the club.

I was up half the night sifting through the police incident reports. After a while I began to see a pattern. Basically the Sharkeys were on the police's hot list, and were automatic suspects for any unsolved cases. Just because they were tagged, did not necessarily mean that the Sharkeys were guilty, or even the prime suspects. But even if they'd committed a quarter of the crimes that they were in the frame for, then they were major players in the criminal underworld.

The crimes were mostly routine stuff, but several reports struck me as unusual because they were not typical crimes. Over the past few weeks it seemed as though someone was targeting Lock's youth for petty, seemingly motiveless crimes. And according to Bernstein's manual, there was always a motive. When you found that, you generally found the criminal. Was Red Sharkey avenging himself on others, just as he had on April and myself?

One of these quirky files was dated September seventh and included a statement from the victim, a Mr. Adrian McCoy. I knew him as a local aspiring DJ. I reread it carefully, taking notes as I went.

I got the decks for my seventeenth birthday. Record decks. Got them sent from Germany, special. You should see the amount of bubble wrap that came out of those boxes. You could wallpaper your house with it. Nothing like them in the country. The arms are balanced down to the last ounce. I don't put vinyl on those decks unless it's been brushed. I make the kids wear surgical gloves when they're mixing on 'em. You never know what those fellas have been scratching, if you know what I mean.

I generally unleash the decks on the public every Friday in the community center. I can mix so smooth you'd barely know you were listening to a different song. The girls love me, or they will when

*I get my braces off. But last Thursday I did the
school junior disco, as a favor to the guys who
idolize me. It was a good night, too, I did a bit of
rappin' myself. I call myself MC Coy, 'cause of my
name. It's clever, isn't it? Well, I think it is.*

*I was a big hit that night. The kids were
all questions about my rig. The dads were
impressed, too.*

*After the show I went out to the van with a
box of vinyl. When I came back someone had
stripped down the decks. They were lying on the
tables like jigsaws. Laid out real neat. Not smashed
or anything. They were fine, except for one thing.
Well, two things. The needles were missing.
Someone took the needles. It's gonna take me a
month to get another set from Germany. That's at
least four gigs, you know. Popular culture in Lock
could collapse.*

*Someone wanted me off the circuit for a
month. That's what happens when you have talent.
But MC Coy will be back better than ever. I'm
using the time to grow my hair a little so I can
have braids put in. In a month's time MC Coy
is gonna tear the community center up like a
hurricane. Not really, you know. Because I could
get in trouble for that and my mom would
ground me.*

I closed the file. Were the youth being targeted

63

for some reason? Was Red the link between MC Coy and April Devereux? Or was someone else behind this mini-spree? I needed more subjects. I opened the next file and began to read.

By the time I called it quits, the birds were whistling outside my window. After half an hour of trying to sleep, I was beginning to take the whistling personally. By the time I dozed off, my curtains were backlit by a dawn glow. I slept on top of the sheets, the bed strewn with sheaves of paper.

I awoke at noon to the sound of metallic pounding. Hazel was starting the weekend at the typewriter, as usual. We would all be subjected to several sonnets on the subject of Stevie before the day was over. I dressed quickly in black, stuffing the Hawaiian shirt deep into the wardrobe.

Mom and Dad were waiting for me at the kitchen table. I could tell by the sudden silence that they had been talking about me.

"How was your little date, honey?"

I selected some fruit from the basket. "It wasn't a date, Mom. It was a business meeting. I'm helping April out with a little puzzle."

Dad put down his paper. "Really? What is it?"

"Sorry, Dad. Client confidentiality."

Dad smiled. "Nice try. Client confidentiality only applies if you're licensed by the state. I want details."

I smiled back, then covered it with a growl.

Sometimes it was a pain having a smart Dad. But I enjoyed our verbal battles.

"April has lost a keepsake that's very important to her. She wants me to find it."

"So what's your strategy?" asked Dad.

I hesitated. If my parents knew the extent of my investigation I would be grounded for all eternity and banned from any activity that contained the letters D-E-T-E-C-T-I-O-N.

"I'm going to conduct a few interviews. See if any of April's friends know anything."

Dad nodded. "Good idea. Did you check behind her couch?"

"Not personally, Dad, but April did."

Mom smoothed my hair. "Did April like the shirt, honey?"

I sighed. "No, Mom. She didn't. There are people in space who didn't like that shirt."

I arranged to meet April and her pink posse by the sports field. This case was getting clogged up with females, and that worried me. In my experience, boys are predictable. As soon as they think of something, they do it. Girls are smarter—they plan ahead. They think about not getting caught.

When I arrived, April and co. were running an unlicensed soft drinks stand.

"You're selling this cola for ten cents a can?" I asked.

"That's right, Half Moon. Do you want one?"

"I suppose. But where do you get the cola?"

April rolled her eyes. "From the supermarket fridge, duh."

I was trying to get this straight. "So you buy the cola for fifty cents a can in the supermarket, and you're selling it for ten."

April spoke clearly, seeing as I was obviously a moron. "Yes, Fletcher, but we don't use our own money to buy it." She handed me a can of cola. "That's ten cents, please."

All I had on me was my ten euro wages.

"I only have a ten."

April plucked it from my fingers. "That's okay. I can break it."

And break it she did, into the largest amount of coins possible.

I took out my notebook and deposited enough change in my pockets to put a strain on my belt.

"So, are you girls in some kind of gang?"

April, May, and their half dozen friends were all wearing T-shirts bearing the slogan *Les Jeunes Etudiantes*. The shirts were pink and had unicorns frolicking around the script.

April seemed delighted to be asked about the group.

"We certainly are. Ready, girls?"

The others nodded enthusiastically then skipped into a ragged straight line. They pointed their toes, placing hands on their hips. All they needed was pom-poms, and I could be at a football game.

"Call us *Les Jeunes Etudiantes*," said April, as though introducing a Shakespearean play. "We find certain things *très intérressantes*."

I winced. Dodgy French rhymes.

> *"Pop stars and fashion,*
> *Movie premieres.*
> *Who's on the red carpet.*
> *Makeup and hair."*

The other girls acted out every subject. *Pop stars* was singing into an imaginary microphone. *Fashion* was a model's pose. You get the picture.

I tried to say something nice. "Hey, that's great. You're really . . . organized."

April made no effort to be nice back. "I wouldn't expect someone from Continentia Nerdia to understand, Half Moon. We're not the kind of people you would normally be allowed to hang around with. Why don't you just ask your little questions and get on with your job?"

I was only too glad to get down to business.

"Firstly, are you absolutely sure the hair sample was stolen?"

April poured cola in a paper cup and stirred it with her finger. "As sure as I can be, Half Moon. I mean, I had it locked in the strongbox in our Wendy house, and next thing I know it's missing. Maybe the dog ate it."

There was a little long-haired terrier skipping around April's shoes. It was obvious from his little pink sweater that he was indeed April's dog. The only non-cute thing about him was the way he bared his teeth at me. I hadn't been having much luck with dogs.

"Do you think he might have?"

"No."

This was going to be a tough interview.

"Did you notice anything else missing?"

May spoke for the first time. She didn't seem as enthusiastic about this investigation as April. "Listen, Fletcher, I know April has a bee in her bonnet about the Shona hair thing, and I know you have an entire swarm of bees in your bonnet about the detective thing. But it's a kids' game, okay?"

I was used to resistance. People don't like to share with detectives.

"So there was nothing else missing?"

"No. Nothing."

I turned to her friends. "So, none of you had something stolen? Or maybe something broken? Something so ridiculous that you thought it must be some kind of accident."

The third girl in line, Mercedes Sharp, raised her hand as though I was her headmaster.

"Well, I lost something last night. I thought I lost it. You know, but maybe . . ."

April glared at her friend. "Come on, Mercedes. You've been moaning on about this mini-disk all morning. This is my investigation. I've already paid Fletcher."

Mercedes returned April's glare, then continued with her story. "I have, I *had*, a karaoke mini-disk that I used to practice my routines for the school talent show. It had everything on it. I had to order it from Japan."

"And you think the mini-disk was stolen?"

Mercedes shrugged. "Maybe. I mean, who would steal a mini-disk out of a player and leave the player?"

"Who can fathom the workings of the criminal mind?" I said, trying to sound intelligent.

"Well, you, I hope," said April. "That is what I'm paying you for. You do have a badge, or so you keep saying."

"Was there any sign of a break-in?" I asked Mercedes hurriedly.

"No," she replied. "But I left my bedroom window open last night. So whoever it was, if there was someone, could have just reached in. Maybe you could swab everyone in the town for DNA."

"Like on *CSI*?" I said wearily.

"Yes. Just like that."

"I'll see if the police lab will loan me their equipment."

Mercedes stepped out of line and reached up to punch me on the shoulder. "Hey, I know sarcasm when I hear it. Watch it, Half Moon, or when I get a boyfriend I'll send him around to your house."

I ignored the ache in my shoulder, checking the list of questions in my notebook. "One more thing, ladies. This is for all of you. Can you think of anyone who might have a reason to dislike you?"

"No," said April immediately. "Who could dislike us? We're popular. You should try it some time, Half Moon."

I let her insults slide off me. I was a professional.

"Well?" I said to Mercedes.

She bit her lip. "Herod asked me to a dance once and April told me to say no. We wrote a little note saying how we would never be caught dead hanging out with a Sharkey. Herod had to get Red to read the note for him. Red got all upset about it. Maybe he took the disk as revenge, like in that story about that prince. . . ."

"*Hamlet*?" I suggested.

"No," said Mercedes, thinking. "*The Fresh Prince of Bel-Air.* One time Will took Carlton's jacket, and Carlton decided to . . ."

April screamed, waving her little fists. "Attention, please! It's Red. We all know it's Red. Why are you wasting time with these stupid questions, Half Moon? Red took the hair, and he probably took Mercedes's stupid mini-disk, which by the way she was not supposed to mention. Stop hanging around here, and go find some proof."

I was beginning to wonder if ten euros was a high enough fee considering all the abuse I was getting, but as Bernstein said: *You don't have to like your employers, you just have to like their money.*

"Red is my prime suspect," I admitted. "But then, everyone is a suspect until my investigation eliminates them."

"That's great," said Mercedes, clapping her hands. "Suspects. It's almost as if someone was murdered."

May had wandered away from the group. She returned now, pocketing her cell phone.

"I like Red," she said in a quiet voice. "I don't think it's fair, blaming everything on him."

May's face was flushed, and she toyed nervously with her hair. My detective's intuition hit me in the gut like a wrecking ball.

"You told Red he was a suspect."

May nodded. "He's on his way over. I just texted him a warning, because he's nice. I didn't think he'd come over."

I thought back to my years studying for the Bob Bernstein badge. The recommended course of action in all situations was to avoid confrontation. Avoiding confrontation was an excellent way to keep your blood in your veins and your bones in one piece.

"Thanks, May," I said, being sarcastic, obviously. "You've been a real help."

May smiled guiltily. "Sorry, Fletcher. You're nice, but so is Red. Pity you're on different sides."

"I hate to spoil the fun," I said, pocketing

my notebook, "but I have some incident reports to chart."

April pointed over my shoulder. "Too late."

I turned toward the playing field. One lanky redhead was heading at speed directly for us.

I felt my throat go dry. "He was playing hurling," I said, my throat clicking as I talked. "How fortunate."

"I didn't know that," said May. "Honestly."

Hurling is the Irish sporting version of pitched battle. The hurl, or bat, resembles an executioner's ax without the blade, and serves roughly the same purpose.

May came out from behind the table. "Don't worry, Fletcher. Red won't do anything. He's nice, really, once you get past the mental bit."

I was not comforted.

Red skidded to a halt before us, kicking up an arc of gravel. He wore faded jeans, and his T-shirt was tucked into his back pocket. He was tall and rangy, bony and muscular. Red's features were sharp enough to cut logs, and his eyes darted like a hawk's, taking in the situation. In one hand he held a chipped and banded hurl. In the other a cell phone.

Les Jeunes Etudiantes were suddenly transformed into Southern belles, half flustered, half delighted. Red had a powerful effect on girls; they either loved him or loathed him. Often both on the same day. I don't know how he did it. A mysterious combination of cockiness and charisma. You couldn't say that Red was handsome, exactly. But whatever he had was better than handsome, because it would last forever.

"I just got a text, Half Moon," panted Red, ignoring the girls completely.

I pulled in my elbows and dropped my gaze. This was the nonaggressive stance wildlife experts recommended adopting when confronted by a gorilla.

"May says you're investigating me. Is that right, Half Moon?"

I could safely answer that one. "Not exactly. You are one of my suspects. Everyone is a suspect until I can clear them."

Red shrugged on his T-shirt. The garment was emblazoned with the slogan *I Fought the Law*. Even his T-shirt was against me.

"A suspect for what? What am I supposed to have done?"

"Maybe nothing," I admitted. "But a lock of hair has been appropriated. Pop-star hair, to be precise."

Red twirled his hurl expertly. It was a vicious length of oak, reinforced at the oval end by a steel band. Red had embossed his name on the band using roundheaded tacks.

"Appropriated? Precise? What kind of freak are you?" Red leveled the hurl at me. "Listen, Half Moon. I have a hard enough time with teachers and shopkeepers and the police, without head cases like you starting rumors about me."

Naturally I wasn't happy about being called a freak in front of a line of pretty girls. But at least I wasn't a bleeding freak. Not yet.

"Breathe deeply, Red," I said, raising my palms to show I wasn't armed. A tip from the Bob Bernstein manual. "By tomorrow you could be off my list for the hair, at least."

Red moved so fast then that I only saw the first bit and the last bit. In the first bit, I was standing with my palms raised and Red was three feet away. In the last bit I was flat on my back and Red was kneeling on the crooks of both elbows. There was barely enough time to be scared, but I did manage to squeeze it in.

"You're not getting it," he said, still reasonably calm. "I don't want to be on or off any list In fact, I want you to burn the list. Leave me alone, Half Moon, or you'll be sore and sorry."

I believed him. Not a doubt in my mind.

May tried to help. She beat Red on the back with an empty cola can. "Get off him, Red Sharkey. You're not impressing anyone. I'm sorry now I tried to help."

Red looked up at May. For a moment something new appeared in his eyes. Something like anguish.

"It's hard enough already, May," he said. "Being a Sharkey is hard enough, with my family the way they are. I'm trying, you know, but what chance do I have with everyone in this town bad-mouthing me? And now Half Moon is jumping on the wagon." He tucked the hurl under my chin like a violin. I could feel it against my Adam's apple. "I'd like to see you try to be me for a day, even an hour. Little weird Fletcher Moon, poking around in other people's business. I bet your biggest problem is which pencil to write with in your stupid little play-detective notebook."

In spite of the situation, I felt anger of my own thumping inside my chest. Don't get me wrong, most of me was terrified, but there is a steel fist of stubborn pride inside me that punches its way out every now and then, especially when someone belittles my profession.

"I could live your life," I grunted, each word a struggle because of the pressure on my throat. "I could go around bullying smaller people. I could steal stuff that doesn't belong to me. And you know what? I'm smarter than you, so I could get away with it, too. But you couldn't do what I do. You couldn't find a clue if it was wearing a T-shirt that said 'I'm a clue.'"

This was a long speech, given the circumstances, and pretty well put together, too. Not many kids would have stood up to Red Sharkey like that. Of course, when I say *stood up*, I don't actually mean stood up literally. Emotions flicked across Red's brow, as though his brain was channel hopping. He went through amazement, fury, and sadness among others, eventually settling on a blank expression that reminded me of the one Mel Gibson did in *Braveheart*, just before he cut some English guy's throat.

"That's what you think?" he growled, and the words did seem to come from the back of his throat. "You think all I do is bully and steal?"

"You think I play at being a detective?"

"It is a game," shouted Red, pulling me to my feet. "A baby's game. You go around playing detective, and innocent people suffer."

I pulled away from him. This was too much hogwash for anyone to bear.

"Innocent people like you, I suppose?"

Red gave me his standard-issue charming grin. "Exactly."

I decided to cut the chase. "Just give me my badge, Sharkey. Give me the badge and the hair thing, and I can close the book."

Red grabbed my shirtfront, dragging me toward him. It was classic hard man stuff, almost an act.

"I didn't take your stupid plastic badge, or the hair. So close the book right now, Half Moon. Close it or else."

Or else what? I wondered, but I never found out, because May's dad pulled up in a station wagon. He opened a window and called to Red.

"Show some backbone, Sharkey. That boy is barely up to your waist!"

Red had never taken orders well. As far as he was concerned this was between him and me, and none of

Gregor Devereux's business. So rather than release me, he lifted me higher until my shirt tightened at the back, and I was forced to rise to my tippytoes.

I often wondered what would have happened then, if Gregor Devereux had been forced to actually rescue me, but it never came to that, because we had a bit of a movie moment.

Something that sounded like a really big lion purred down the street. I looked over my shoulder to see a large, gold, 70's BMW pull up to the footpath, almost nudging the Devereux station wagon. This was the Sharkeys' car and everyone in town knew it. It had been doing the rounds of Lock since before I was born. Local legend had it that Papa Sharkey won the car from a millionaire German tourist in a game of *boules*. Legend also had it that the lock on the driver's door was broken and Papa never bothered to have it fixed, because no thief would be stupid enough to steal Papa Sharkey's car.

The front window came down smoothly, and a huge head dipped into the light. The face was mostly wild black beard, with two laser-blue eyes that calmly took in the situation.

"Get in the car, son," said Papa Sharkey. "We're going to the grave today."

His voice was impossibly deep and smooth. Like someone had mixed the bass guy from a soul band and the guy who does the movie trailers together in a vat of treacle. A voice like that was difficult to disobey, but maybe Red had practice, because he held on as tightly as before.

Papa spoke again, his tone a shade harder.

"Red. In the car. Now."

Red glowered for a moment, then swallowed it. He shot me one last loaded look, then released my shoulder, crossing the road to the BMW. He climbed inside the dark interior, and the car pulled away slowly. I didn't take my eyes off the big sedan until it cut through the estate and out of sight. It would be about three hours before my heart slowed to normal speed.

Mr. Devereux got out of his car and straightened my shirt. "Steer clear of that one, young Moon. He's trouble. Just like the rest of his family."

I was inclined to believe it. The police files confirmed that the Sharkeys were indeed trouble. It seemed as though Red was following in the family footsteps, in spite of May's faith in him.

"Thanks, Mr. Devereux."

Mr. Devereux slapped a patch of dust from my shoulder. "Call me Gregor. What was that all about, anyway?"

May began loading the stall into the back of the Volvo. "Red is a suspect."

Gregor Devereux collapsed the legs on the folding table. "Maybe you should just leave that alone, Fletcher. It's not worth the trouble for a lock of hair."

I was surprised to find that I was as pigheaded as my mother always said. "I can't do that, Gregor. I've already been paid, so I have to see this through. And anyway, it's not just the hair anymore. There's something strange going on in Lock."

Mr. Devereux sighed through his nose. "Oh, really?"

"Strange little thefts. Mini-disks, record player needles. I need to know why someone would want all these things."

"I see April has signed you up for Paranoia 101," said Mr. Devereux. "Okay. It's your hide. Are we ready, girls?"

April was a million miles away. Probably imagining herself walking down the aisle toward the pop star of the day.

"April, let's go. May has to practice her dancing. The school show is next week. This year we're coming home with the trophy. That will show her mother."

April blinked back to the real world, then ran around to the passenger side, catching my sleeve on the way past "Keep me up to speed."

I nodded, watching the Volvo full of pink-clad girls draw away.

Up to speed? Suddenly, everyone's a detective.

That night, back in my office—I say office, but it's actually my bedroom that I think of as an office. It sounds better if you say to a client: I'll need to run a few tests back in the office, rather than: I'll have a look at this with a magnifying glass after I put my PJ's on.

Officially I was asleep, but actually I was working the evidence. Twenty minutes past Cinderella's curfew and I was still trawling through the police reports. September seemed to be a busy month for the Sharkeys. Maybe they were getting a head start on their Christmas list

I had scanned an ordinal survey map into my iBook, layering it over a hundred-square grid. Then I mapped each crime onto the grid using a color-coded system. It took a while, but eventually I had an overview of suspected Sharkey activity in Lock. I studied the plottings for a while and realized if the Sharkeys had actually committed all these crimes then they must be operating twenty-four hours a day, every day. There was the option that they had people working for them. Not all the sharks had to be Sharkeys.

Something rustled outside the house, startling me. I turned off the bedroom light, dropping my gaze to the back garden. After a few moments, my night vision kicked in and I could make out the familiar shapes of walls and bushes. One of the bushes seemed to be moving. Unusual. It was unlikely that I was witnessing the birth of a new mutant species of bush, so I concluded that there was someone behind the plant.

I was correct. Seconds later a hooded head popped from the foliage. This was followed by an arm, which beckoned me down. Strange. Why would someone wish to talk to me at this time of night? Someone roughly my own age, judging by the height.

It's perfectly reasonable, I told myself. You are a detective on a case. Everyone knows about the investigation, thanks to May. This person lurking in the evergreens must have some sensitive information.

I made sure I had my notebook, pulled on my jacket, and resolved to make my e-mail address more widely available in future so this kind of skullduggery wouldn't be necessary.

My parents were in bed, having had a rough day raising their children. Hazel was in her bedroom acting out all the parts in a new play entitled *Not So Happy Now, Are You?* It was a simple matter for me to sneak downstairs.

I did pause for a moment, listening to the voice of reason inside my head screaming: *Are you insane? Don't you watch horror movies? Go back upstairs.*

But I was a detective. How could I turn away from this development? Even so, I thought it best to play it safe and take a shortcut through the garage. Maybe I could get a look at my snitch before he got a look at me.

I padded across the kitchen and through the adjoining door to the garage. I had been this way so many times that I picked my way through years of junk without causing the slightest clatter.

One slipped bolt later and I was in the garden, crouching behind Dad's prized gnome. Dad's gnome looked pretty traditional, but when Hazel accused him of being old-fashioned, he claimed it was a post-modernist ironic gnome that was mocking its own heritage.

I heard footfalls nearby, and peeked over the gnome's pointed hat. A huge mistake, as it turned out. Something sliced through the darkness at speed, heading directly for my head. A club of some kind, definitely being wielded as a weapon. I heard the prowler grunt from the effort, like a tennis professional serving for the match. No sooner had I raised my hand to protect my face than it was pinned to my forehead, and everything above my neck seemed to be on fire. The force of the blow lifted me six inches from the ground, sending me sailing into a rock garden.

I lay there unable to do anything except wonder why the stars were going out one by one. I still had the darkness, but no more stars.

DR. BRENDAN'S BEDSIDE MANNER

I WOKE UP ALONE, which I felt was highly unfair. I had always known that someday I would be knocked unconscious; it went with the job. But for some romantic reason I had believed that when I came to, there would be a crowd of concerned family members and admirers hovering around the bed. But there was nobody. Just a sterile hospital room.

The pain was something else I hadn't bargained for. Every time I moved, it felt as though brain jelly was seeping out through cracks in my cranium. There weren't, in fact, any fractures in my skull, just bone bruising. A very cheerful doctor explained this to me when he arrived much later on his morning rounds.

"Did you ever see those movies where the bad guys kick the devil out of the good guy?"

"Yes."

"Well, that's what happened to you."

Dr. Brendan would have been a dead man if I could have raised my head without squealing like a schoolgirl. Obviously he thought I was four years old.

"The point is," continued Dr. Brendan, "that those movie guys aren't really hitting each other. In actuality."

"You don't say."

"No really, I'm serious," continued Dr. Brendan. "It's all pretend. Human beings aren't built to take that kind of punishment."

I closed my eyes, hoping he would go away.

"A knock like you got. Well, you're lucky to be alive. Okay, you don't look so good, right now, but most of the damage is just deep bone bruising, except for the nose. Your left hand took most of the force."

I opened my eyes. "What was that about my nose?"

"Snapped like a wishbone. We're going to be setting it this evening. And your hand was pounded like a raw steak. Nothing broken, but you won't be playing the violin for a few months."

"My head is ringing."

Dr. Brendan checked my ears with a penlight. "An aftereffect of the trauma. But again, it's tempo-rary."

In my mind's darkroom, a picture of Franken-stein's monster began to develop.

"You'll be on painkillers after the operation. Maybe you should get a pair of dark glasses, too."

"Why? Will the light hurt my eyes?"

Brendan giggled guiltily. "No, just to stop you from looking at yourself in the mirror. You're going to be quite the troll for a while."

"Troll?"

"I'm afraid so. For at least two months, ugly is going to be your middle name. And quite possibly your first and last name, too."

I moaned. Several bubbles popped in my nose.

Dr. Brendan took pity on me. "I'm sorry, Fletcher. I thought a joke might get your spirits up."

"Spirits up!" I groaned, each syllable sending a laser burst of pain through my nose. "Are you crazy?"

Dr. Brendan hooked my chart on the bed's foot rail.

"No no," he said gallantly. "Just doing my job."

Dr. Brendan held up a few fingers, then decided that I wasn't concussed and went to fetch my family from the hall.

Mom nearly passed out when she saw my bruised face.

"It's not as bad as it looks," I assured her, trying my best to smile. From the look on my mother's face, I guessed that smiling made things worse.

"Oh my God, Fletcher," she cried. "When we

found you, we thought you were dead. Hazel heard a noise, and your Dad went outside. What happened? Tell me."

I told the absolute truth. "I saw someone in the garden, so I went outside. I was attacked with a hurl or bat and I woke up here." I tried to put a brave face on it, but most of my face was buried beneath a mask of bruises.

Mom wanted to cradle my head, but she had to make do with hugging an imaginary head eight inches to the left of the real one.

"This is terrible. In our own garden. Outside our own door. And you, you fool, going outside in the middle of the night! Some detective you are."

The sympathy was drying up fast.

"Yes," agreed Hazel. "Don't you ever watch horror films?"

She held out a small tape recorder. "By the way, could you describe exactly how you felt at the moment of impact? I'm writing a short story . . ."

"Put that away, Hazel," hissed Mom. "The poor boy is in pain."

Hazel persisted. "Would that be a white-hot pain? Or more of a dull, throbbing pain?"

Dad cut across my sister's research.

"Is this anything to do with your investigation?" he asked me.

"Maybe. I don't know. All I was doing was looking for a missing keepsake."

"Well, whatever. This investigation is over, as of now. We put up with this detective bit because it was harmless. I won't ban it completely, because I know it's your passion. But from now on, all cases go through me. Understood?"

I nodded gently. There was no point in arguing while everyone was so emotional. I could present my case at a later date when I wasn't sporting a face that would cheer up Quasimodo.

Hazel took something from her pocket when my parents weren't looking.

"I have something for you," she said, holding it up so I could see. Lying in her palm was my notebook.

"You dropped this in the garden."

"Thanks, Sis," I said.

That evening Dr. Brendan was having difficulty telling the difference between over-tens and under-fives.

"Want a lolly?" he asked.

"No. Thank you. You don't by any chance have a pacifier?"

The doctor frowned. "No. But I'm sure one of the nurses . . ."

"I was joking. Just trying to keep my spirits up."

"Good soldier. Now let me explain what's going to happen when we knock you out."

Dr. Brendan took a nasal splint from his pocket.

"Now, young man. What do you think this is?"

"It's a nasal splint."

"No. It's actually a . . . ah, yes, you're right. It is a nasal splint. You're a clever one, aren't you?"

"There was a module on emergency first aid in my diploma course."

Dr. Brendan was phased. "You sure about that lolly?"

"Yes."

"Anyway, your nose has to be set, and one of these put on. The swelling has gone down quickly, so we're going to do that now. Obviously, you don't want to be awake when I start hauling your broken nose into line, so were going to inject some sleepy potion . . ."

"You mean anesthetic?"

"Erm . . . Yes, anesthetic, into your arm. And when you wake up, everything will be okeydokey."

"That's just wibbly wobbly wonderful, Doctor." My private-eye patter was really coming on.

Dr. Brendan searched my battered face for signs of sarcasm. I'm sure he found plenty.

"I'm sure it won't hurt, too much."

I had no smart answer to that.

They lifted me onto a gurney and wheeled me down to the operating room. An anesthetist stuck a drip in my arm and pumped in a syringe full of white liquid.

"Now, Fletcher, count backward from ten to one."

I did so. Slowly.

"You still awake?" asked the anesthetist, who looked about seventeen.

"Nope," I replied.

Dr. Brendan had dropped the kiddie lingo. "Fletcher is a real brainiac, you better give him a little extra just to stop those thoughts spinning around his head. And if he stays asleep longer than usual, I'm sure no one will mind."

The anesthetist took a larger syringe from his tray. This one looked about the size of a German sausage.

"Are you sure?" I asked, alarmed. I decided right then and there to stop being funny with medical personnel.

"I know what I'm doing," said the anesthetist. "I *am* in my second year in college, you know. Now, count backward from ten."

"Ten," I said.

A person has vivid dreams under anesthetic. My mind replayed the events of the past twenty-four hours in glorious Technicolor and surround sound.

I could hear vague conversations and crunching noises coming from the world outside my head, but I decided to ignore these because I suspected the crunching was being caused by my own nose being hauled into line.

Time passed and a theory emerged. The

sequence of events seemed simple enough: I am hired to investigate the Sharkeys. May tells Red Sharkey about this, and so he decides to do something about it. The *something* being attacking me in the middle of the night. But I had no proof that Red was my assailant. Or had I?

If it was Red Sharkey who attacked me, then he had probably used the same weapon as he had to threaten me earlier. His hurl embossed with his own name. His own name!

I woke up in the recovery room and immediately tried to fill the nurse in on my theories, but she merely stroked my forehead with a cool hand until I had no choice but to go asleep again.

I woke up for the second time. Sort of. My head was awake, but my body was pleading for sleep. I ignored it. This *Red* idea needed to be acted on now. Tomorrow would be too late. The proof would be lost in a pool of blood.

I had no idea what time it was. Night. It was dark in the room but I could see a slit of light under the door, and hear the slap of nurses' rubber-soled shoes in the hall.

I sat up in bed. Too quickly. I felt as though my head was balanced like a ball in a cup, and would plop off if I jiggled too much. I was back in my own hospital room now, and the nurse was gone. Nobody to lean on.

Take it slow, then. I swung my legs onto the cold

floor, testing my strength. Weak but steady. The walls seemed to be flexing slightly, like fun house mirrors. That was the anesthetic. In all probability, the room was not spinning.

I stumbled into the bathroom, grabbing on to anything I could to support me. One of these things was the radiator. It could have been hot. I wasn't sure. My fingers were still buzzing from the anesthetic.

The bathroom was cramped, which suited my lack of balance. I could lean against a wall and still face myself in the mirror. But did I really want to face myself? Did I want to see what had become of my head? Would I recognize the battered remains of once-normal features?

With a swollen head, it might be hard to see how severe my injuries actually were. Dr. Brendan had assured me that I was fine, apart from the nose. But my eyes felt like two marbles in a ball of jelly. A ball that could split its skin at any moment. Maybe I should just go back to bed.

Before this idea could take hold, I grabbed the light cord and yanked. After a moment's wincing, I focused. It was not a pretty sight. Dr. Brendan had been right, ugly was going to be my first, middle, and last name for quite some time. In fact, the best looking thing on my face was the nasal splint, a small aluminium V clamped onto my nose. The rest of my features looked as though someone had dropped a pound of rare steak onto my face, and it had stuck.

"Focus," I told myself. I had to act now, or the evidence could be lost.

My left arm was bound from elbow to knuckle in a soft cast. I tugged on the Velcro straps with my teeth, all the time arguing with my sensible side. The pressure eased, and my arm seemed to expand like an inflated rubber glove. I expected some pain but none came. However, beyond the anesthetic, I sensed that my body was screaming at me just how stupid this idea was.

I slipped off the cast with my good hand. My left arm was even uglier than my face, which was saying something. The single blow had managed to connect with every inch of skin facing the weapon. I forced myself to study the bruising. There were several colors, from sickly yellow to angry red. And running from my wrist to my hand, a deep purple trio of distinct marks. My evidence.

I held my arm to the light. And there in the mirror was my proof. Three letters. R.E.D. The round-headed tacks on Red Sharkey's hurl had etched their signature into my arm.

My detective's brain accessed my file on bruising. Bruises fade quickly. Sometimes in hours. This purple bruising would quickly soften and spread. I needed to preserve the evidence before it blended with the rest of the tissue damage. There must be a way.

Of course, in a perfect world, I would simply press the call button and tell the nurse that I needed a digital camera immediately. But I knew from experience that adults did not react well to boy detectives. The nurse would more than likely look at me as though I had two heads and one of them was purple. I would be bundled into bed and possibly sedated until the bruising had faded. On top of that, I would be lucky to wake up without a child psychologist in the room.

I would have to do this on my own. I found my sneakers and a hospital gown in the closet. It took a minute to get the sneakers on, because my feet felt like they belonged to someone else. I scolded my toes as though they were misbehaving infants.

"Now, now, boys. Keep still. Good little piggies."

A part of my brain realized that the anesthetic still had a grip on my good sense, but the rest of me had evidence to process and was determined to be professional.

The hallway was clear. I could hear conversation on the wards, but there was nothing but floor tiles between me and the nurses' station. I strolled across confidently, as if I had a medical reason for being there. The station was bordered by a semicircular counter, and behind that a few worn chairs. There was an extension cord on the floor. Plugged into it were a kettle and a photocopier.

I switched on the copier and waited, shuffling impatiently while it heated up. At last the red light flashed green. I pulled back the lid and plonked my arm on the glass. That really should have hurt, and probably would later, but at that moment I felt no pain.

I made a copy. But it was worthless. No court in the world would admit it as evidence. The image was blurred and the reversed letters were barely visible. I tried again, darkening the picture. Still no good. Now my entire arm was coming out black.

This was ridiculous. In this age of technology, I was being thwarted by a Stone Age photocopier. I needed a digital camera. Right now. Maybe it was my imagination, but it seemed as though the incriminating bruises were already fading. If only my family were here. Hazel's cell phone had a built-in camera. But if I removed my cast in front of my mother to take a photo of a bruise, she would have had a nervous breakdown on the spot.

May Devereux had a camera connected to the computer in her Wendy house. And I knew where the key to the Wendy house was. The Devereux house was barely a minute from the hospital. In fact, Rhododendron Road was clearly visible from the main entrance. I could just saunter over there, snap a few quick photographs, and nip back to bed before anyone knew. In my fuzzy mind, this plan made perfect sense.

I belted my hospital gown, thrust my injured arm deep in the pocket, and pushed through the double doors into the reception area. In my semi-anesthetized condition I decided it would be a good idea to sing a quiet little song, so as to appear casual and certainly not up to mischief. Unfortunately, because my brain was buzzing so loudly, I sang like someone wearing headphones. Out of tune. And louder than I intended.

"To all the girls I've loved before," I warbled. My Dad's favorite, forever on the CD player in the kitchen. *"Who've traveled in and out my door."*

A nurse blocked my path. She glared at me the way you might look at something that has crawled from a sewer leaving a trail behind it.

"Excuse me, *Julio*," she said, hands on hips. "Would you mind reining in the voice? There are babies being born in this hospital. We wouldn't want the first sound they hear to be your painful howling. There could be lawsuits."

I would have been hurt, if I hadn't already been hurt.

"Of course, nurse. I'm so sorry. I get carried away sometimes."

"This could be one of those times if you're not careful. Now, on your way. And keep the noise down, or I may decide to check your temperature, and believe me you don't want that."

The threat was accompanied by a steely grin, and suddenly having my temperature taken seemed like the scariest thing in the world. I scurried to a waiting area and pretended to be engrossed in a *Beautiful Homes* magazine.

"What're ye in for?" said a man beside me, a ragged line of stitches running across his forehead.

"Ingrown toenail," I replied, thinking he was joking. After all, my injuries were as plain as the nose on my face.

"Oh," he replied. "Sore yokes, dem."

"Yes. Terrible."

I checked that the nurse had gone, and scampered out the front door, very quickly indeed for someone with an ingrown toenail.

It must have been very late, because there wasn't a car on the road. I nipped across and leaned against a gate post on Rhododendron Road. The fresh air was not perking me up like I thought it would. In fact, I felt dizzy and nauseous. No throwing up, I warned myself. Especially not on clients. That would be very unprofessional.

The gate to May's house was open. I crept in, sticking to the grassy verges to avoid crunching the gravel underfoot. Pretty smart thinking for someone suffering the aftereffects of anesthetic.

A fine mist pattered on to my head from the fountain. They must have gotten it fixed. The water was most refreshing, so I opened my mouth and tried to catch a few drops.

I caught sight of a shadowy figure in an upstairs window. Even in my foggy state it was clear that it was not

May or indeed her father, unless one of them had sprouted a beard since we had last met.

I was immediately concerned. Was this my attacker? Had he moved on to his next victim? My heart pumped faster.

Who was this mysterious bearded man, and what was he doing in the Devereux house? It was too late to conceal myself in the bushes. I was standing under the moonlight in a pool of white gravel. There was only one approach to take. The direct one.

"Who are you?" I shouted, the words vibrating inside my fragile head. "What are you doing in there?"

The shadowy figure pressed against the glass, beard hair spreading like a halo.

"If you've done anything to May, I will find you."

The window creaked open, and a tremulous voice drifted down to me.

"If you're looking for May Devereux, she lives next door."

I was, of course, outside the wrong house.

I retreated sheepishly, bowing slightly as if that would help. My little trip was no longer a secret. No doubt the person in the window would be burning up the phone lines between here and the police station as soon as I was out the gate. I had minutes before a couple of boys in blue came to drag me back to hospital.

I hurried next door, trying not to let my head wobble too much. The dizziness was worse now, and I wanted nothing more than to lie down in the rose garden and have a little rest. Perhaps if I went to sleep here, I would somehow wake up in my own bed.

Just a few more minutes and I could rest. Record the evidence, then back to bed. Two minutes at the most.

Two minutes would have been plenty if something hadn't caught my eye. The entire side of May's house was glowing a flickering orange. There was a fire somewhere nearby. I loped around the corner, feeling slightly duller than a jelly knife.

I heard the fire before I saw it. Pistol-crack flames and boiling hiss. Black smoke filled the garden, rolling in thick coils from a bonfire near the Wendy house. I staggered closer, trying to see what was being burned. All I could make out was the elbow crook of a sleeve, glinting with golden thread.

I gasped with sudden horrible recollection. May's Irish dancing costume had gold thread.

She could be in the fire, I thought. May could be in there.

"Fire!" I screamed, and my head nearly exploded. The pain drove me to my knees in a bed of roses.

"Fire!" I howled again, and the unlikely combination of pain and anesthetic shut my entire body down for a few crucial moments.

I awoke to find myself somehow closer to the fire. Alive then, but only barely, judging by the pulpy feel of my skull. I staggered to my feet, working up to a sprint to the Devereux's side door. Please, God, let May herself answer my knocking.

I reached up to check my nasal splint, and realized that there was a blackened stick in my hand.

That doesn't look too good, I thought.

That was when two of Lock's finest hurdled the garden wall and buried me deeper than the flower roots.

CHAPTER

6

IN THE PUBLIC EYE –
AND NOT IN A NICE WAY

WHEN I WOKE UP in my hospital room, Chief Inspector Francis Quinn was perusing a copy of *Woman's Way* from the magazine rack.

"Knit one, purl one," he was mumbling when I sat up.

The chief was as close as it was possible to be to a human bulldog, just not as cuddly. He had black eyes buried in his head like driven nails, and red jowls that wobbled when he was talking, as he was now. I knew it should be impossible, but I had always thought that the chief slightly resembled his wife, Principal Quinn.

In spite of my situation, my mind began to drift.

I began seeing things. Suddenly Chief Quinn had a trident in his hand. It suited him.

"You have sinned, Moon," he roared. "And now you are mine, and I will rotate your soul on hell's barbecue for all eternity!"

A great fiery pit opened up below my hospital bed.

"So you think you're tough?" continued Quinn. "We've got boys down here that will roll you up in a ball and play hurling with you. Then when they've finished, I'm going to rub your raw soul in salt and toss it to the hounds."

And then we fell down, down, down, and all I could hear was the demonic laughter of Chief Francis "Lucifer" Quinn.

Okay. So maybe some of that didn't happen.

"Fletcher!" shouted the chief, bring me back to reality, where I definitely did not want to be. "Are you listening to me?"

I struggled on to my elbows.

"Yes. Oh my God, is May all right?"

Quinn frowned. "Of course. I suppose she'll miss the costume, but her daddy can easily buy her a new one."

Costume. I sighed in relief. Just a costume.

"Good. That's great news. Did you get the arsonist?"

Quinn swiveled a chair, straddling it.

"Oh, I think we did. We got him, all right."

"Well, who was it?"

There were two officers flanking the door, and they threw each other incredulous looks. Eventually the chief spoke.

"I'm looking at him."

It was a simple enough statement, but somehow it wouldn't take root in my head.

"What?"

"The arsonist. I'm looking at him. We all are, except you."

So, everybody in the room was looking at the arsonist, except me. Therefore the arsonist was in the room. And the arsonist was . . .

"Ah, hold on now a second."

Quinn rested his chin on his arms.

"Watch this, guys. The denial of the century, coming up."

I backpedaled along the bed. "I'm the arsonist? Me?"

"Oh! A confession. That was easy."

Quinn lit a fat cigar, sucking like he was trying to siphon gasoline.

"I am innocent."

"That may be true," admitted Quinn. "But I have to play the percentages. A known nosey parker is found at the scene of an arson attack actually holding the smoking torch. Obviously in your twisted mind, May Devereux is responsible for the attack on your person yesterday, so this is your revenge. You are a lucky boy that no one was hurt."

My life. Where had it gone?

I allowed myself six more words. "I want to see my lawyer."

Of course I didn't actually have a lawyer. I'm only twelve, for heaven's sake. But I thought Quinn might back off a few steps if he knew legal representation was on the way. Of course he shouldn't have been talking to me at all without my parents present.

Five minutes later my parents were present, and they did not look happy. What they did look was distraught and furious at the same time. Mom assured me that everything would be all right, fondly tugging my little toe, which was the only part of me not aching after my "arrest." Dad paced the room, threatening everything in it, including me and the furniture.

"Forget what I said earlier," he said. "From now on investigating is completely banned. Your license is revoked. You are a twelve-year-old boy, Fletcher. When are you going to start acting normally?"

That hurt more than my broken nose. I knew I was a bit different, but never thought of myself as abnormal.

"This is normal," I whispered. "For me. I can't make myself good at sports."

Dad stopped pacing. "That's not what I mean. I don't want you to be me. You can be yourself, but couldn't you do that without the cloak and dagger?"

Mom tugged my toe. "Come on now, Fletcher. Promise us you'll forget all about this silly investigation."

I opened my mouth and nothing came out but air. How could I make a promise that I couldn't keep? I had to know what was going on here. Curiosity had me in a vise. With every breath I thought about the case.

I was saved by the arrival of the family lawyer, Terry Malone. He handled all the family paperwork, then I checked it for mistakes. If Terry were Santa Claus's lawyer, then Christmas would be doing several life sentences for breaking and entering.

"Well, okay then," said Terry, once he had switched on his recorder. "Let's go over this story again."

I sighed. "Last night I was assaulted outside the house. I had a theory that Red Sharkey could be responsible so I ran across to May's house to photograph the evidence."

"Which was?"

"A bruise spelling out his name. Backward."

Terry fished a disposable camera from his tweed jacket pocket.

"Could we see this bruise?"

Mom's knees almost give out. "You most certainly could not," she shrieked. "It's under the cast."

"Oh," said Terry, disappointed. "So what made

you decide to torch May's dance costume? Do you have a history of pyromania?"

"I did not torch anything," I spluttered indignantly.

"Of course you didn't, honey," said Mom, slapping the lawyer's shoulder. "Why would you say that, Terry?"

"You know what the police are like," said Terry innocently. "Arguing over every little point. Anyway, I was hoping Fletcher would tell me the truth this time."

"I am telling you the truth!" I protested, a touch too shrilly.

"Well then, why were you roaring and screaming outside the neighbor's window?"

"I was at the wrong house."

"Do you really expect anyone to believe that you went to the wrong house, when you visited the correct house only the day before yesterday?"

"It was dark. They both had fountains." Weak. Pathetic.

"Okay," sighed Terry. "Let's move on. How do you explain the fact that you were found beside the fire holding a torch?"

That very same question had been gnawing at me.

"He must have put me there."

"Who?"

"The *real* arsonist. Keep up, Mr. Malone." I was

starting to sound guilty, even to myself.

"Okay, okay. So, the arsonist dragged you to the fire, then what?"

"Then he put the torch in my hand and left me for the police."

Terry consulted his notes. "That's what you told me on the phone. At least you can keep your story straight. You wouldn't believe how many of my clients can't tell the same story twice."

"It's not a story, it's the truth."

Terry smiled wistfully. "If I had a penny . . ."

The throbbing in my head moved up a few cycles.

"Their case is flimsy," I said. "There's no real evidence."

Terry winced. "Apart from motive, means, opportunity, fingerprints, and DNA."

I cracked momentarily. "What do you want, Terry? Tell me and I'll give it a go. Do you want me to pull a rabbit out of my splint as a witness? Or maybe I could rewind time and we could have a look at the action replay? How about that?"

I'm ashamed to say that I followed this outburst with a bout of hysterical laughter. Not just little chuckles either—these were big lusty howls. When I had recovered sufficiently to peep between my fingers, Terry was regarding me with new respect.

"Insanity," he said. "I like it."

JAILBREAK

AFTER A FEW DAYS OF suspicious looks from the nurses, Dr. Brendan took off my splint and cast.

"No concussion," he declared. "And the X-rays for skull fractures came back negative. Did you ever see those movies where the bad guys kick the devil out of the good guy?"

"I did," said Sergeant Murt Hourihan, who had come to pick me up that evening.

"Well," said the doctor. "That's what happened to Fletcher."

Murt had to sit down he was laughing so hard. It didn't strike me as funny. Then again, I'd heard it before.

They sat me in a wheelchair and rolled me down the hospital corridor. I felt like Hannibal Lecter on tour. Nurses and interns lined the walls whispering things like *Don't let him near the matches*. I was happy to be leaving, even if it was for an interview in the police station.

My parents had agreed to a formal interview provided they could be present along with Terry Malone. After this interview, Chief Quinn would decide whether or not there was enough evidence to send a file to the Director of Public Prosecutions. I was hopeful that this entire mess could be cleared up in a couple of hours.

Murt's squad car was parked across the ambulance bay by the main entrance. I transferred myself from the wheelchair to the backseat. Murt took off at speed, honking impatiently at a line of elderly patients on the crosswalk.

We pulled onto Rhododendron Road, passing May's house on the right. She had not come to see me in the hospital. Why would she? May probably thought I was the lunatic who burned her dance costume. And even if she didn't believe that, her dad had surely crossed me off the list of welcome visitors.

"George Montgomery is filing a complaint, you know," said Murt over his shoulder.

"Who?"

"Colonel George Montgomery. The Devereux's neighbor. He's filing a complaint. He phoned Quinn at home right after you showed up outside his house."

I groaned. "I thought I was in . . ."

"Yeah yeah, May Devereux's garden." Murt blew out noisily through his nose. "What's going on, Fletcher? Are you going through some kind of rebellious phase?"

I sat up. "No. Of course not. This is all a mistake. Red Sharkey assaulted me. He probably started the fire, too."

"Red Sharkey. Right. We questioned him. He was at home the entire night. His family backed him up. As a matter of fact, his father requested protection in case you go after his son next. But about the assault, we found his hurl in the next garden to yours. With any luck we'll match the blood and fingerprints, so we should get him for that at the very least, but you're definitely in the frame for starting fires."

My nose was throbbing. "This is ridiculous, Sergeant. You know me. You can't believe any of this."

Murt shrugged. "It doesn't matter. As far as Quinn is concerned the case is solved. Your file is already gone to the Director of Public Prosecutions."

"That's not fair," I blustered. "He was supposed to wait until after the interview."

"Well, the chief didn't want to miss the last mail pick-up. Don't worry, Fletcher, we're not beaten yet. I won't give up my best civilian consultant so easily."

Murt cocked his head suddenly, sniffing the air.

"Do you smell that?"

Moments later I did. Wisps of black smoke were floating through the air vents. Murt sniffed the fumes.

"Oil line I'd say. There's a leak somewhere and it's coating the engine."

"Is that dangerous?" I asked.

"Absolutely," said Murt conversationally. "The whole engine could go."

He pulled over to the footpath, double-parking on a white line. "All out."

Murt opened the security door and set me sitting on the path twenty feet away from the vehicle. The smoke was billowing from under the bonnet now, engulfing the entire car.

Murt winked at me. "I presume I can trust you not to run away, Fletcher."

I half laughed. I barely had the energy to stand up, never mind run away.

The smoke was thicker now, almost solid. It didn't seem to bother Murt. He strode into the middle of the cloud, rolling up his sleeves. No doubt he sucked down worse every day from the cigars in the interview room.

It never occurred to me that I was being busted out of custody. Things like that just didn't happen in Lock. Nobody had been rescued in our town since Father Gannet Roche had broken young Bill the Butcher Turner out of reform school to play in the county hurling final.

It finally dawned on me what was happening when a mountain bike skidded to a halt by my feet. I looked up to see a rider who was wearing a striped ski mask.

"Get on the back, Half Moon," he said. The voice was all too familiar.

"Sharkey!" I gasped.

"Could be," said the figure.

I picked up some gravel from the gutter and threw it at him. The stones jingled harmlessly through the spokes.

Red rolled up the ski mask. "Honestly, you try to help some people."

"Help!" I spluttered, too indignant to be scared. Almost. "You attacked me. You set fire to May's garden. This is a dry month. That could have spread."

Red swung off the bike, kicked the stand and hunkered down before me.

"Look, Half Moon, I heard about the letters on your arm, but my hurl was stolen, okay? Someone wanted me to be blamed. The same thing is happening to you. I know you're too wimpy to set fire to a garden."

"Thanks."

"Don't thank me. It's not a compliment."

"I didn't really mean it."

The sound of Murt swearing at the engine drifted up the road wrapped up in plumes of smoke.

"We have to go," insisted Red.

I wasn't convinced. "How can I believe anything you say? All I ever get from you are insults or threats. Your entire family has a history of theft, fraud, and assault."

Red glanced toward Murt. "Forget all that, Half Moon. If you get back in that car, it's all over. Your big investigation is finished. Whoever is messing with us will get clean away with it."

"Us?" I asked.

Red rolled his eyes. "I'm rescuing a parrot, heaven help me. Yes, *us*. You, me, April, May. Us."

Curiosity sliced through the weakness and uncertainty. True, this person had threatened to harm me, but if I went to the police station, then I would be blamed for the fire and the real culprit would get away unpunished. And if Red *had* started the fire, why would he want to rescue me when I was all set to take the blame? This question needed an answer.

"Why, Red? Why would you want to help me?"

Red dropped his eyes. "I felt bad about shoving that hurl at your throat the other day. I blew my fuse."

This was all very noble, but there must be more. "And?"

"And if this assault charge sticks, I could end up in juvie this time. I can't let that happen." I saw anguish in Red's eyes for the second time. "This is not the way I want my life to go, and it's going that way anyway. I thought if I just stayed out of trouble, then

I could be my own man. But Sharkeys are like trouble magnets. You're the one who got me involved in all this, so you can get both of us out. You're the detective."

My instincts told me that Red was telling the truth, but there was something between us that I couldn't let go.

"If I'm going to be a detective, I'll need my badge."

Red studied an ant on the pavement for a moment, then dug the badge from his pocket, tossing it on the road between my feet.

"Sorry," he said, still looking at the ground. "I lost my head. I shouldn't have taken it, I mean, you *were* right. Herod did steal that organizer, even if he won't admit it."

I picked up my badge and polished the face on my shirt. Just having it in my hand made me feel smarter.

Down the road, Murt Hourihan discovered that someone had put an oily rag on his engine. He balled the rag in his fist, flinging it to the ground. His first thought was that this was mindless mischief. His second was that there was a purpose behind it.

The policeman pulled his head out of the smoke, squinting toward his charge. "Hey!" he spluttered. "Hey, what's going on there?"

Red rolled down his ski mask. "Coming or going?"

Murt was running now, legs pumping under him. "Last chance, Half Moon. Was all that detective talk just talk, or are you the real thing?"

"Don't you move, Fletcher!" shouted Murt, his voice rough with smoke. "Stay right where you are."

Red kicked up the stand. "I bet your file has already gone in. I bet the PTA is already having an emergency meeting at the school, making sure you won't be a bad influence. That's what they do, you know."

This was all happening too quickly. I liked to think things over. Make my deductions at a leisurely pace. Was any of this really happening? I flexed my fingers and the pain ran all the way up to my nose. It was happening, all right.

Red stared out from the eyeholes in his mask. "I didn't do it, Half Moon," he said. "I took the badge, and I'm sorry about that. But I never attacked you, or set a fire in May's garden."

Red held out his hand.

"There's a mystery here, Half Moon. I know you can solve it."

Mystery. The magic word. I took Red's hand and he swung me onto the seat of the bicycle, like a cavalry officer rescuing his fallen comrade.

I held on tightly as Red put his weight on the pedals, building enough speed to outpace Murt Hourihan. Pain pinged my nose with every bump in the road.

"You pair of good-for-nothings!" wheezed Murt. "Get back here or there'll be hell to pay."

Hell to pay. The phrase stayed in my mind long after the sound of Murt's wheezing had faded in the distance. I had just escaped from police custody. There *would* be hell to pay. And I was the one holding the bill.

CHAPTER

AT HOME WITH THE SHARKEYS

RED TOOK THE LONG WAY home, dragging me across several fields and a stream before he finally doubled back to his own house. By the time we reached Chez Sharkey the sun was painting the undersides of the clouds a deep orange, and anyone under the age of ten was being tucked in for the night.

Chez Sharkey was the most famous house in the southeast. It had once belonged to the American filmmaker Walter Stafford, but he had lost it in a poker game to Red's grandfather. Over the years, the surrounding estate had been built up by developers, but the old house remained untouched. It stood proud yet ramshackle, a mock Tudor mansion in the middle of a dozen almost identical housing estates.

"This place must be worth a fortune," I whispered as Red freewheeled down the back path.

Red shrugged, which is dangerous on a bike. "Maybe. Papa would never sell. Mom loved this house."

Red's mother had died several years previously. I still remember the day he got the news in lunch hall. Red had kept right on eating his sandwiches. Then, when he'd finished the last one, he crumpled the tinfoil and threw it in the garbage. We didn't see him for three months after that. As far as I know, nobody had ever asked Red how he was feeling. He wasn't really a touchy-feely group-hug kind of person.

We dismounted from the bike in a yard of cracked paving stones. Weeds clawed their way through every crack, and at least a dozen cats hissed at our passing. The back door was massive and black. The edges were chipped to reveal rainbow stripes of glossy paint beneath. A century's worth of layers.

Red stowed his bike by the wall, then put his shoulder against the door. He was still wearing the ski mask, and I got the feeling he was comfortable in there.

"I haven't cleared this with Papa yet, Half Moon," he said, rolling the woolen cap from his face. "So you stay out of sight until I do."

"Out of sight? I thought you had a plan."

"I had the first part. The breakout. I thought you could handle the rest of it, bright spark."

"My name is Fletcher, Red."

"Oh, really? And what's my name?"

I waited for my brain to supply the information, but it didn't come. I had no idea what Red's actual name was. He'd been Red since we were little.

Red winked at me, his point made. I had no idea what that point was, but as far as Red was concerned he had definitely made it.

We crept into the house. The ceilings were high, and faded wallpaper curled in the corners like pages from an old book. Red pushed me into a room.

"Just stay in there until I come and get you," he whispered. "There's a bed in the corner. The light doesn't work, but that's okay, because you probably want to spend your time thinking." He handed me a disposable cell phone. "Here, take this; there's no call credit, but you can send texts. The number is withheld so nobody can call you back."

The door closed slowly against a buffer of air, and I was alone in a dark room in the house of someone I wasn't sure I could trust. I felt a sudden welling of panic in my stomach. What had I done? I was a fugitive hiding in the lion's den.

I lay on the bed and all my aches and pains came rushing back. The dregs of prescribed painkillers were still swilling around my system, but only enough to make me sleepy. I held the phone's screen close to my face like a candle, and with numb fingers I typed out a short message.

HZL, I M OK. TELL M+D NO 2 WORRY. HOME SOON. MST FIND ARSNST. LUV U ALL. FLETCHR.

I sent the message to Hazel's phone, then switched off. What had happened to me? This was not the way detective stories were supposed to go. I was supposed to be in my office, bent over my desk, examining the evidence. That's how Bernstein described it in the manual. But the manual wasn't the real world. This was the real world here and now, and I had dropped myself directly into the deep end without ever pausing to test the waters.

I threw the phone across the room then closed my eyes against the darkness. I kept them tightly closed for a long time, until eventually I fell into a deep sleep haunted by dreams of raging fires and broken bones.

I woke sometime later to see sunlight glowing through my eyelids, highlighting the veins. The warmth felt good, so I lay there savoring the sensation. Peace at last. A quiet moment in which to plan my investigation.

Something tugged on my toe. I looked down. A small, filthy child was slipping off my shoes. The boy was a miniature version of Red, with fiery hair and a wiry frame. It was Herod before his weekly wash and brushup.

"What are you doing?" I croaked.

Herod glared back undaunted. "You're dying. What would you want shoes for?"

"I am not dying, go away!"

Herod straightened to his full height, the crown of his head barely cleared the mattress.

"You go away. This is my house. Buttercups, my eye."

I wrestled my shoe from his grasp. "I will go away, far away. Bet on it. And next time you stash your booty, watch where you step."

I sat up slowly, and was surprised to find my head remained relatively pain free. Now that I could see the room's decor, I decided that the headaches would probably come back if I stayed here much longer. The bedcover appeared to have been cobbled together from a thousand other bedspreads, every one of them luminous. The walls were that particular bright green generally associated with the Caribbean, and the curtains seemed to be fashioned from some type of metallic foil.

In the light of a new day, my escape seemed utterly ridiculous. The police would have listened to reason. After all, I was a respectable student from a respectable family. Not anymore, I argued with myself. I had abandoned my studies and my family. And all to solve a mystery. Now there was no way back into my cozy life, except by solving that mystery.

"I thought you were leaving," said Herod, chewing absently on a wart on his knuckle.

"Don't worry. I'll be gone soon enough. I just need to talk to Red. Where is he?"

The boy jerked a thumb over his shoulder. "In

the kitchen. They're waiting for you. The three of them."

This piece of news filled my stomach with acid bubbles. The Sharkey clan was waiting for me, and probably not with hot chocolate and croissants.

Herod left the room and I followed, deeper into the house. With every step, my own world seemed further away. The walls were old-house high, covered with ancient thick wallpaper that was coming loose at the top, curling over us like a rain-forest canopy.

We turned off the dark passageway through a rectangular doorway of light, into a stone-flagged kitchen. The Sharkeys were gathered around a huge pine table digging into heaped plates of sausage and bacon. I stood quietly, and for a brief, happy moment, nobody noticed I was there.

Then Herod cleared his throat noisily and three Sharkey heads swiveled slowly in my direction, like tank turrets. I knew every inch of their faces. I had read files on all of them. Nobody was smiling.

Red winked at me. He was going for jaunty, but all he looked was worried.

Papa was there of course, massive and hairy, a wiry beard sprouting just below the eye line. His police file was as thick as a redwood. Papa had been involved with every caper from ticket scalping to lobster poaching.

Red's big sister, Genie, was there, too. Strikingly beautiful, with the trademark Sharkey red hair and lack of fashion sense. She had once been the lead singer with a girl band called Sharkey Attack. They had managed to build up quite a following on the local circuit. That was, until Genie had socked an admirer with a microphone, knocking out four of his front teeth.

"Morning," I said weakly.

Papa stood. He was so tall that all I could see was a belly and a beard. "This is him?" he boomed in his movie-trailer-guy voice.

Red nodded. "Yes, Papa. This is Half Moon—I mean Fletcher Moon."

Papa loomed over me, shaking his head, as if he couldn't believe what he was seeing.

"This little speck of a thing is *investigating* me?"

Red jumped from his seat, tugging on his father's sleeve. "It's not really investigating. It's more play-investigating."

Red winked at me. *Go along with it*, the wink said.

"Is that right?" Papa asked me. "Play-investigating?"

"Yes," I began, then felt my badge dig into my thigh. "No, actually. It's real investigating. I have a badge and a notebook. And if I were you and I had me on my case, then I'd be worried."

Papa frowned. "Well, if you were me and you were on my case, then you'd be chasing your own backside." This observation was followed by a huge bark of laughter that would have scared off a pack of wolves. Red laughed too, in relief. I tried to chortle along, but all that came out was a trickle of Morse code squeaks.

Papa's laughter petered out, but its ghost remained. He didn't see me as a threat. I didn't mind. A lot of adults make that mistake.

"Sit," he boomed.

I sat.

"Hungry?" he asked. I wasn't sure if he wanted to feed me or eat me.

"Half a grapefruit would be nice."

Genie piled a plate high with fried pork, spinning it along the table like a Frisbee. It rotated before me for several seconds, spraying my shirt with grease.

"Or sausages would be nice, too." I said, attempting a smile.

I ate slowly, feeling four pairs of Sharkey eyes boring holes in my skull. Nobody spoke, and my chewing seemed louder than a farmer striding across a field of mud.

For a while I cared about this, then I realized that I was famished and that the sausages were delicious. I devoured three rapidly, the third wrapped in a slice of soda bread.

"Shy little chap, aren't you," said Papa when I had finished.

"Sorry," I mumbled. "I've only had hospital food for the past few days."

"Oh, yes, that's where you told the police that my son assaulted you."

"That's what I thought at the time," I said into the remains of my breakfast.

Papa sat at the head of the table, staring at me from under eyebrows that would have thatched a fair-sized cottage. His serious face was back in full force. "And now?"

"And now I think that probably both of us have been set up. Red for the assault, me for the arson."

Papa popped a jumbo sausage into his mouth. It barely hit the sides on its way down.

"I don't see what this has to do with me, Half Moon. The police have been setting us up for years, and now all of a sudden I need some kind of midget detective to help me out. A midget detective who said that this entire family has, and I quote, 'a history of theft, fraud, and assault.'"

The last lump of sausage stuck in my throat.

"It sounds bad when you put it like that," I admitted. "In my defense, you do have a history of theft and fraud. I may have been wrong about the assault."

Papa bristled. "Theft and fraud?"

I suddenly felt invulnerable, as though this was all a dream. "Well, there was the time Red fed white bread to Byrne's greyhounds before a race."

Red sniggered. He couldn't help it, even though he was trying to turn over a new leaf.

"Not to mention the time Herod stole the duck race machine from Tramore carnival."

"Quack, quack," said Roddy.

"And Genie was collecting money for her Confirmation until she was eighteen."

Genie winked. "I'll be going out next year, too."

"Shut up, you lot!" roared Papa. "I'm jittery enough with this chap in the house."

Red tugged his father's sleeve again. "Papa, if I don't clear up this assault thing, they could take me away. I know that I've been in fights before, but no Sharkey would ever sneak around in the night beating up midgets like Half Moon. Don't underestimate him, though. He's titchy, but he's as sharp as a razor. He nailed Roddy fair and square for stealing Bella's organizer."

Herod slapped the table with both hands, his face distorted in a scowl. He looked like a redheaded monkey.

"I did not take that stupid thing!" he objected. "Half Moon set me up. I was framed!"

The Sharkeys laughed, all except Herod.

"Of course you were," said Papa. "If I had a penny for every time you said that, I'd buy the Dublin Spire and feed the parking meter for a month with the change."

Papa picked up another sausage, waggling it at Red. "The two of you have twenty-four hours to play Sherlock Holmes. After that, Half Moon goes home. His parents must be losing their minds. I don't want to be accused of kidnapping, along with everything else."

I frowned. Twenty-four hours. Not a lot of time to clear up a major case.

"I'll need my stuff. My laptop and notes."

"Not a problem," said Red, looking slightly shifty. "Follow me."

He led me down the hall past a dozen Sacred Heart lamps, into the end bedroom. Unlike the room where I had slept, the decor was quite tasteful. In fact . . .

"This is my stuff!" I shouted, gathering my duvet in my arms. "You burgled my house!"

"I thought you might need your detective gear," said Red. "I told Genie and Roddy only to take your computer, and any maps or files. They got a bit carried away."

I grabbed a reading lamp. "They didn't hurt anyone?"

"No. Your parents were out looking for you last night. It was perfect."

I felt as though my heart had turned to ash and a good breeze would scatter it irretrievably. I had caused my parents pain.

"I need to go home," I whispered.

Red took the lamp gently. "In twenty-four hours, Half Moon. As soon as you've solved this case."

"How can I solve anything?" I asked, feeling desperate and alone.

Red shrugged, heading back to the kitchen. "You're the detective, Moon. Detect something."

I followed him, spreading my arms. "I can't set foot outside the front door without being arrested."

Red wiggled his eyebrows, as though he was the man with all the answers. "I have a plan."

"What plan?" Suddenly I was nervous.

"Actually, it was Genie's idea. We were working on it all night. It's simple. You become one of us. A Sharkey. No one will look at you twice."

I didn't like the sound of this plan much. "I don't think that's going to work."

Genie was suddenly fluttering around me like a shop assistant.

"Of course it will," she said. "Your tan is coming on nicely."

"What tan?"

Genie took my hand and led me to a full-length mirror. It barely registered that the mirror was from my own bedroom.

"You look like one of us already."

Terror took hold of my gut. I couldn't look.

"Go on," said Genie. "It's not that bad."

That might have been encouraging had everyone not collapsed in fits of giggles.

"Oh, no, please no," I said, because I had looked.

Someone had cut my dark hair while I had slumbered in a deep painkiller-induced sleep, and what was left of it was dyed red.

And that wasn't the worst of it. Dangling from

my left ear was a large silver pirate hoop. Genie flicked the earring with a spangled nail. It pinged.

"Sign of quality," she said. "I think it suits you."

My complexion was several shades darker than normal. I tried to rub off the color, but it refused to shift.

"Hollywood Glow fake tan," explained Genie. "It's a bit patchy because I didn't have time for moisturizer. That stuff won't wash off for at least a week. Your elbows and knees may be brown for a few weeks. It says on the box not to use it on the facial area, but if you're not burning by now, then you're probably okay. Okay?"

My nose was still swollen, and between the dyed head, the swelling and the new color, I was a different person.

Genie rolled up my shirtsleeve, revealing a tattoo on my forearm.

"Don't have a freak attack, Half Moon," she said when I began hyperventilating. "It's only henna. It'll wear off in a few weeks."

I lifted my arm, and read the tattoo. "'Don't X me?'"

"Don't cross me," corrected Genie, slightly miffed. "It's a cross."

I was grateful that my other arm was in a cast, or heaven knows what the Sharkeys would have done to it.

Red elbowed his way into my reflection, draping

an arm around my shoulder. "Do you remember at the sports field? *You* said that being me would be easy?"

I nodded. I remembered.

"Well, now's your chance to prove it." Red held me at arm's length, grinning. "Welcome to the family, Half Moon."

I hadn't just bent the rules of investigation, I had stomped on the manual, shredded the pages, and burned the strips. Instead of being the discreet detective on the shadowy outskirts of the case, I had become the case. My involvement was changing things. Now my own future depended on the outcome. This case was no longer just a job; it was my life.

I tried to concentrate on the facts, but images of my parents crept into my thoughts.

Twenty-four hours, I told myself. Twenty-four hours.

If I didn't use the day to solve this crime, then I would always be seen as the crazy Moon kid who went around starting fires and playing detective. I decided to do what I always do when life won't leave me alone. I lost myself in my iBook.

The Sharkeys had broadband. Not because they paid for it, but because they were piggybacking on a neighbor's wireless modem signal. I opened my Internet browser and logged on to the police site. In a few keystrokes I was downloading all the September cases that were not related to the Sharkeys. I hadn't done this at home because it would have taken hours with a regular modem and tied up the phone line. With broadband it took less than five minutes.

I searched through the files, looking for something unusual. Something an adult might view as trivial. I speed-read for half an hour until the phrase "chocolate report" caught my eye. That was nothing if not unusual. I opened the file and read the following statement:

Complainant: Maura Murnane. 18 yrs. Female.

I had been off the chocolate for ages. Six months and three days, that's half a year. The trick is to avoid the stuff. There was none in the house. I never went shopping alone, and Mom made me leave the room during commercials. I was in the local paper as Slimmer of the Year.

Chocolate. I was off it. Staying away from it. Then one day, it just started showing up. I woke up and there was a Mars bar on my pillow. I thought I was dreaming. I closed my eyes, but when I opened them again there it was. Looking at me like a chocolate kiss. Like the sweetest good morning you ever had. I jumped out of bed and ran downstairs. I thought it must be a joke. My little brother, maybe. Not a chocolate bar at all. Otto is like that. Once he

tied my dog to a bus fender. Mom threw the Mars bar
away, but the next morning there was another one.
And the next, and the next. It was like the chocolate
fairies were stalking me. But I resisted. I was very
good. So Mommy moved into my room, to try and
catch whoever was planting the Mars bars. But there
were no more Mars bars. And I thought that was
the end of that, until one day at lunch, I made a
sandwich. Brown bread, lean ham, and low-fat
mayonnaise. I left it on the table for a minute, a
second, but when I bit into it—ten seconds later, I
swear—the ham had been replaced with After Eights.
They were lovely, even with the mayonnaise. I've
been hooked on those sandwiches ever since.
Mayonnaise and After Eights.

There was a note underneath tagged on by the
investigating policeman.

> *This is not a priority one case. The girl's mother*
> *made her complain. Possibly Maura is sneaking*
> *herself chocolate, and invented this mysterious After*
> *Eight man to stay out of trouble.*

I, on the other hand, was not so sure. Another
one of Lock's youth had been hit in the weak spot.
The list was growing: April, May, Red, MC Coy,
Maura Murnane, and of course, me. There was a conspiracy here. I was certain of it.

The Sharkey children obviously watched too much television. They gathered around my computer, expecting me to unravel this riddle with a few strokes on the keyboard and a knowing look.

"I have to go out," I said.

Red headed for the bedroom. "I'll get you some of my old clothes."

Genie was disappointed. "Don't you want to build a profile?" she asked.

"With what?"

"With all the evidence that you downloaded from satellite surveillance, obviously. Don't you watch *CSI*?"

I ground my teeth. "I need to visit the crime scenes first, before they get even more contaminated."

Herod punched Genie on the shoulder. "Moron. He has to visit the crime scenes."

Genie swatted her little brother with a hairbrush. "I know that, Roddy. Don't touch the jacket. I haven't cut the security tag off yet."

Red returned with an AC/DC T-shirt and a purple tracksuit. The tracksuit was so shiny that it seemed to crackle with static electricity.

"Put that on," he said, throwing me the bundle. "It's time to test your disguise."

We left Chez Sharkey on foot, because two boys on a bicycle would fit the description doubtlessly being circulated by the police. I pulled the tracksuit sleeve well down over my cast.

There was a policeman leaning against the front gate pillar, on stakeout just in case the dangerous fugitive Fletcher Moon decided to wreak revenge on his attacker.

The officer on duty was a Cork man. John Cassidy from Cobh. He had once consulted me on a spate of burglaries across the bridge. I'd pointed him in the right direction and charged him a box of Maltesers. Cassidy had only spoken to me once, but he was a policeman and trained to recognize faces. Even ones covered with fake tan.

"Remember," Red whispered out of the side of his mouth. "You're a Sharkey now. People will treat you differently."

My plan was to sidle past Officer Cassidy with a hand shadowing my face. This was not Red's plan. He wanted to put my disguise to the test. He grabbed my elbow, steering me right into Cassidy's line of sight.

"Hello, Officer," he said, grinning broadly. "Have you met my cousin . . . eh . . . Watson?"

Watson? Oh, very funny.

Cassidy grunted. "Watson, is it. You Sharkeys certainly do pick names. Genie, Herod, and Watson. I have to ask, Red. Why Herod?"

"Mom wanted something Biblical. It was her last wish. Herod was all she could think of at the time."

Red's eyes were looking somewhere else. Into the

past, where his mother was alive and made the house a home. For a long moment he was distant, then his trademark jaunty grin flashed back.

Cassidy turned his attention to me, and I felt as though there was a flashing arrow over my head with my real name written on it. He gave me a slow once-over.

"Just don't go robbing anything while you're in town, Watson. I don't know how things work wherever you're from, but here in Lock we take a very dim view of vagrant criminals."

I was dumbstruck. This policeman had accused me of being a thief without knowing a thing about me, except that I was a Sharkey.

Red elbowed me in the ribs. Cassidy was waiting for a response.

"Okay, Officer," I said sullenly. "I'll stay out of trouble. No problem."

Cassidy gave me his version of a scary stare.

"Just see that you do, or you'll have me to deal with."

We were eye to eye, and there wasn't a flicker of recognition. People see what they expect to see.

"I'll have to deal with you."

"So long as you understand that, we'll have no problem."

"Not a problem in the world, Officer."

And just like that, Fletcher Moon was invisible, hidden beneath an earring and a tracksuit. Watson

Sharkey, however, was all too visible, and branded as a thief before he even opened his mouth to speak. Was this what being a Sharkey was like? If it was, I couldn't wait to become a Moon again.

There was a line of cars outside the Moon house. Mom's Mini, Dad's Volvo, and a police blue-and-white. Through the net curtain I could see my mother sitting on the couch, her face whiter than her favorite emulsion, Arctic Snow. Dad was there, too. I caught sight of him as he paced past the window. A human pendulum. But the image that will always stay with me was the moment Hazel entered the room. She asked for something. A drink, or permission to use the house phone, and my Dad exploded. He turned on her, shouting, until she retreated up the stairs. Dad never shouted. Hazel never retreated. What was I doing to my family? Could it ever be undone?

Red punched me on the shoulder—his version of encouragement.

"Keep it together, Half Moon. They can either be sad for twenty-four hours or forever. You've got a job to do, so get on with it."

Twenty-four hours or forever. Twenty-four hours would seem like forever, at the very least. Better get on with it. Time to be a professional.

I nodded tersely. "Okay. Around the back."

There was an eight-foot concrete wall running

along the side of our house. Hazel and I were absolutely and utterly forbidden to climb it, and had been doing so since we were five. Red and I scaled the wall using well-worn hand and footholds. It took me longer than usual with my injured arm. A single crow stood sentry halfway down. The bird played chicken with us until we came too close, then rose in a squawking black flurry of feathers. To me the crow sounded louder than a full orchestra, but nobody came out to check on the commotion.

I dropped down beside the very bushes where my attacker had hidden. Red landed beside me, very quietly. Like someone used to prowling. It struck me that until yesterday, he had been my prime suspect.

"Been here before?" I asked him, forcing a smile.

"No," said Red. "If I had, I certainly wouldn't be here now."

I thought about that for a second and couldn't find a single reason why Red would return to the scene with his victim. Unless, of course, he was insane.

"Had any checkups recently? You know, with a psychologist?"

Red raked his fingers through the grass. "If you're not going to search for clues, I am."

I caught his wrists. "Stop it, Red. You're destroying evidence."

Red leaned back on his haunches. "Okay, detective. Detect."

I studied the area behind the bush, where my

attacker must have waited. I didn't touch anything, just looked—sweeping my eyes across the ground like twin scanners. It had rained since the assault, so most physical evidence would have been washed away. But maybe there was something.

I found my something tucked in tight at the bush's base. A single huge footprint.

I pointed it out to Red. "Look, a print."

Red blinked. "That's huge. Who is this person? A clown?"

I felt suddenly scared. "This is the biggest print I have ever seen. It must be a foot and a half from toe to heel. This person is a monster."

We squatted there for a moment, staring at the print, imagining the man that left it. I don't know about Red's imagination, but mine was running riot, dressing the man in a black cape and covering his face with scars. He probably had an eye patch, too, and a hump.

"Where are the other prints?" asked Red. "Did this guy just pogo down from space on one foot?"

"The rain," I explained. "It washed away the trail. This print was protected by the bush."

Red pulled out his cell phone and used the built-in camera to photograph the print.

"Just preserving the evidence," he said.

I smiled. "You're learning."

In the Bernstein manual there is a short chapter on undercover work. The first line says, in capital letters,

AVOID UNDERCOVER WORK. Bernstein goes on to say that an undercover assignment is the most difficult type of detective work. This is because it often forces the detective to go against his nature and pretend to be something he isn't, i.e., a normal person. If the criminal under investigation suspects that the undercover operative is not "a stand-up guy" and is possibly a "rat fink stool pigeon" then statistically the undercover operative has a mere fourteen percent chance of survival.

Encouraging stuff. Especially since I was undercover as a member of a criminal family. Double whammy.

Our next stop was another recent crime scene. Mercedes Sharp's house. I needed to find a connection between my assault and the missing mini-disk. If there was a link, then I would know we were after a single perpetrator. Or a single group of perpetrators.

As we passed through Lock's housing developments, I tried to imitate Red's swagger, become a Sharkey. Red had a way of walking that made him look cool. Everything he did, from opening a can of cola to running his fingers along a rail, looked cool. It would take me several lifetimes to perfect that. When *I* opened a can of cola it looked as though I was afraid it would explode, which it often did.

"What are you doing?" Red asked. "Did someone kick you in the behind?"

I decided, foolishly, to tell the truth. "I'm walking cool. Like you." I wiggled my fingers theatrically. "Being a Sharkey."

Red raised an eyebrow. Just one. "Being a Sharkey? Listen, Half Moon. Being a Sharkey is not something you can learn in a day. You might fool an adult, but not a kid. Just stand behind me and hope nobody notices you."

I shot Red with a finger gun to show that I understood.

"What was that?"

"It was, you know, a finger gun. It means loud and clear. Ten four."

Red sighed. "Thank goodness for that. I thought you were about to start picking your nose."

I stopped trying to be cool after that.

Mercedes's house was empty. Her father owned the local paper, and her mother was editor-in-chief, so both were probably out beating doors to find me. The house was an old detached building with wild ivy scaling the walls and weeds clawing their way through cracks in the flagstones.

"Nice place," commented Red.

"If you like jungles," I said. "Lucky for us, the Sharps like a natural-style garden."

"Why is that lucky for us?"

"Because the crime scene should be relatively uncontaminated, except by the weather."

We slipped down the side path around to the back of the house.

"I wonder which is Mercedes's window?" said Red.

It didn't take long to figure out. There were six windows at the rear of the house, but only one had the word *Mercedes* spray painted on the glass.

"I'm guessing that one. Whoever took the mini-disk must have been grateful."

"Mercedes has a sister, you know," Red pointed out.

"Your point being?"

"My point being, Half Moon, that the sister probably lifted the mini-disk. That's what sisters are for."

"Good point. We'll check on that later. Somehow."

There was a flower bed at the base of the wall. Just a bed. No flowers. It seemed as though they had been ripped out.

"Signs of a search," I noted, scribbling it down in the notebook that the Sharkeys had thoughtfully stolen from my room. "Someone really went through this."

"Maybe a gardener?"

"No. We've got rose stalks here, and ferns. These aren't weeds. Someone was looking for something."

I pulled back a sheaf of withered ferns. Below it was a second giant footprint. A connection. For a

moment I felt light-headed. Here was the first con-
crete proof that there was a link between the crimes.
And where there was a link, there was a pattern.
Bernstein. Chapter six.

"Red. Can you photograph this?"

Red held the phone at arm's length. "This guy is
big, Half Moon. Maybe too big."

Red was right, but I didn't care. I had the scent
in my nose. There was a connection and I was right.
The truth might hurt, but it was the truth, and I
would find it.

"We have no choice," I said. "Either he's the
criminal, or I am."

I swept the area for more clues, but in all honesty
we were lucky to find the footprint and evidence of a
frenzied search. We were about to pack it up when
something scraped on the gravel behind us.

"Red Sharkey?" said a voice. "What are you, like,
doing?"

I knew who it was before turning. A private
detective does not forget the voice of his first cash
customer. April. I kept my head down, using Red's
frame as a shield. Through the crook of his arm, I
could see her. April was dressed as perfectly as ever, in
a pastel pink tracksuit, a matching lunch box dangled
from one hand.

Red was calm under pressure. I got the feeling
he was used to being under pressure.

"Hey, April. I was walking past, thought I saw

someone suspicious coming around the side. Me and Watson, my cousin, thought we'd check it out."

April didn't swallow a word of that. "I was right about you and your family. Here you and your little friend are snooping around Mercedes's garden. Maybe you were snooping around May's garden, with a torch."

I stepped into the open. It was time to find out if I still had an employer. "Red wasn't there, April, but I was. The torch wasn't mine, though."

"What do you mean?" asked April. Then the penny dropped, from a great height and with a loud clang. "My God, Fletcher. Is that you? What happened?"

I tried to get in the essential information. "It's me, April. I just want you to know that I had nothing to do with May's dress."

But April was still trying to get to grips with my appearance. "But your hair. It's gone, and red. And your nose, my God, your nose. And you have an earring now! And a tattoo!"

April stepped closer, completely forgetting that I was definitely a fugitive and possibly an arsonist. "Is that food coloring in your hair? Tell me that's not a real tattoo. And that tracksuit. Those colors are all wrong for you."

Then it dawned on her that she was sharing space with two dangerous criminals. Her mouth formed an 'O,' but no sound came out.

Do not spook a scared animal, says Bernstein. The same principal applies to humans on the edge. No loud noises, no sudden movements and no big gestures.

"April," I whispered, keeping my hands by my side. "Red and I. We're both innocent. Red broke me out so that I could prove it. There's something going on in Lock, and I have to find out what it is. You, Mercedes, May, Red, and I. We're all victims. And there are more. I don't know how many yet. You know I could never set a fire at May's house."

"So what were you doing in her garden in the middle of the night?"

Good question, and difficult to answer without sounding like a lying criminal.

I chose my words carefully. "There was a bruise on my arm after the attack. It spelled out Red's name, backward. I needed to photograph it with May's digital camera. The dress was on fire when I got there."

This was so preposterous that April took a step backward. "You wanted to photograph your bruise? Is that the story you're going with?"

I shrugged. It was the truth. What else could I say?

"And you two are working together. Red Sharkey and Fletcher Moon are a team? I'm not paying any extra."

"I'm not taking the blame for any of this," said

Red, kicking a pebble. "If Half Moon can get me out of trouble, I'm prepared to put up with him for a short period."

Obviously we weren't best friends just yet.

"So what did you find out?"

"We established a link between the assault and the robberies. The same person was responsible for both."

April snorted. "I already know that. So which of you was it?"

"Not us. Someone bigger than us. A lot bigger."

A car crunched over the gravel driveway out front.

"That's Mercedes and her Gran, home for lunch," said April. "Right on time."

Red grabbed my arm. "We have to go. Now."

I looked pleadingly at April. "Don't say anything. Just for one day."

April was in control and she liked it. I knew from the smirk on her lips that she wouldn't turn us in, just yet. Having us under her thumb would be too much fun.

"One day. Though you're going to feel pretty stupid when it turns out that Red really did take Shona's hair."

There were doors slamming now. I could hear Mercedes complaining at the front of the house.

"April. We have a contract. You can trust me."

April spent half a second thinking. "I doubt it.

There's a hole in the hedge on the left. It brings you out behind the school."

I nodded, then bolted for the hedge. Red was already a shadow on the other side of the branches. As I squeezed through the foliage, I heard Mercedes squeal as she came around the corner. For a moment I thought she had seen me, then I realized that this was how Mercedes said hello.

9

PROOF, OR RESULTS?

BACK AT CHEZ SHARKEY, Herod had a car door propped up against the garden wall.

"Go!" shouted Genie, clicking the button on a large stopwatch.

Herod pulled a flat metal ruler from the leg of his jeans, sliding it between the window and frame. He jiggled the ruler for a few moments and the car door lock popped.

"Clear," he shouted, stepping back.

Genie stopped the watch. "Fifteen seconds. Not bad. Keep practicing."

She noticed us coming through the back gate.

"Ah, will you look who it is. Well, boys, any developments in the case?"

"We've established a link between the assault and the robberies," replied Red. The exact words I had used with April.

"Well put," I said.

Genie held out the stopwatch. "The clock is ticking, boys. Better get back to business. Red, you haven't rehearsed since this mess started, and we have a title to defend."

I followed Red into the house.

"Title?"

"School talent show. I was Elvis last year. The Early Years. This year I'm doing Vegas."

I remembered. Another reason why the girls loved Red. He could sing, and even more important, he *would* sing.

When we reached the bedroom, my iBook's browser was open on an Internet shopping page.

"Were you on the 'Net?" I asked Red.

Before he could answer, Genie pushed into the room past us.

"I was—just buying some clothes from Paris," she explained, quitting the site.

"Don't you need a credit card for that?"

"I have one," she said, tossing me the plastic rectangle. "Maxed-out, I'm afraid."

This didn't bother me much, until I noticed the name on the card.

"That's my dad's!" I blurted. "You stole it from my room."

"Hey, we're family now, Watson. What's yours is mine."

"But this card is for emergencies only."

Genie hopped up from the chair and grabbed my waving hands. She waltzed us both around the room. "It *is* an emergency, Watson. The autumn-winter season is upon us and I'm still wearing spring-summer clothes."

I was still twirling when Genie sneaked out the door.

"You need to watch my sister," commented Red, steering me to the chair. "She'd steal the ham out of your sandwich."

I ran a quick virus sweep on the iBook and found that Genie had managed to infect the hard drive with a minor virus. I ran the disk repair program, hoping that none of my files had been corrupted. Red sat, watching the program run for about four seconds before his natural energy began bursting out through his extremities. First his knee began jittering, then his toes, then his fingers drumming a beat on the desk.

"Red, please."

"What?"

"I'm working, here."

"I'm not stopping you. Anyway, what work? You're looking at a screen. How long are you going to be?"

I shrugged. "I don't know. Why don't you go play a game of hurling?"

Red elbowed me. "Someone stole my hurl, detective."

I unstrapped my cast and laid it on the desk. "That's right. How could I forget?" My arm was still bruised, but the pain only flared if I clenched my fist. So, I avoided clenching my fist.

Red's entire being was eager for action. "There must be something I can do."

I pointed at the mass of files on the floor. "Those are the September case files I have to go through. If you could weed out a few red herrings that would save us a lot of time."

"Red herrings?"

"Our criminal is in there somewhere, but so is every other criminal in Lock. We're looking for unusual crimes with no obvious motive, possibly teenage or young victims."

Red thought for a second. "Okay," he said, scooping the files into his arms. "Give me a few minutes."

A few minutes? It had taken me hours to get through the first half of the pile.

"Good luck. But investigation is slow work. It could take a while."

"We'll see, Half Moon," said Red, pulling the door closed behind him with his foot.

Red seemed to take the energy out of the room when he left. I suddenly felt incredibly tired. I felt as though I'd been beaten inside and out. Which of course I had. I put my head in my hands and tried to fend off thoughts of home. At the very least my family would be feeling as bad as I was. Was this what being a detective entailed? Where were the lightning flashes of intuition that I had expected?

The computer beeped and I sat up. All·clear on the hard drive. I selected Office Works and began to work up profiles of each victim. Maybe once they were in print, then I could find some connection between them—assuming that Red wasn't the connection.

I dedicated a page to each subject, filling it with every scrap of information I could find. I topped each page off with a photograph, which was surprisingly easy to find on the school Web site or local paper archives. I didn't bother with a photo of myself, as I know what I look like, and I knew I wasn't guilty.

I got one of Red from an Elvis impersonator competition publicity photo. I downloaded a photo of Maura Murnane from the local paper's online archive from when she won Slimmer of the Year. MC Coy had his own Web Site, featuring blurry shots of himself in various tracksuits. And there was a lovely one of May and April on the school fun page.

Red barged back into the room. He had been gone less than twenty minutes. Poring over files was not for everyone.

"I'll be with you in a minute."

Red pulled my chair away from the computer. "I think you better come now. Papa is solving your case for you."

That got me out of my seat fast. I did want the case solved, but I was surprised to find that I didn't particularly want anyone else to solve it. At the risk of sounding like Arnold Schwarzenegger, this one was personal.

I spoke to my computer. "I'll be back," I said, then chuckled at the joke that only I understood. Which, I believe, is one of the first signs of insanity.

Papa was seated at the kitchen table with the files piled high in front of him. In one hand he held a statement, in the other a cell phone.

"Petey," he said into the phone. "That tire job below in Doyle's garage. I'm presuming that was you and the boys, was it?" Papa winked at me, which looked pretty much like a bear winking at a salmon. "I thought so. Why? Oh, nothing. I might be in the market for a few radials, that's all. Talk later."

Papa hung up, tossed the file into the garbage, and moved on to the next one. There were already several files in the garbage.

"Has Papa already phoned those people?" I asked Red.

Red seemed almost embarrassed. "No need. Papa knows exactly who committed those crimes. He was nearby at the time. Very nearby, if you know what I mean."

I could guess. After all, some of those were the Sharkey files.

Papa was on the phone again. "JoJo. I see you've been up to your old tricks again. What do you mean what do I mean? The fruit truck in Wexford. You're the fruit man in this county and everyone knows it. How about a few boxes of kiwis? I'm very partial to kiwis. Good man. I'll be over tomorrow."

Another file in the trash. Some files didn't even merit a phone call.

"Jimmy. Bob Hooley. English Ned."

All files in the trash.

This was not how Bernstein said things should be done. There was no proof, no secondary confirmation.

"Do you have a shred of proof?" I asked Papa. "Eh . . . No offense."

Papa ripped a file in half. "Proof, Half Moon? Proof? Do you want proof, or results?"

I thought about the accusations painted on my head like a target. I imagined the hourglass of time running out, and I thought about my family, worried sick.

"Results," I said.

"Good. Give me five minutes."

Red threw together some sandwiches while Papa worked. We stood at the sink eating.

"What's next, Half Moon?"

I chewed this over, along with a strip of chicken. "Next, I suppose, we find our mystery giant."

"Shh, moron," hissed Red. "Do you think Papa is

going to let us run around town after a giant? Keep that to yourself."

"Keep what to yourself?" asked Papa, who apparently could hear a whisper at the other side of the room.

Red tossed out a quick lie. "His bad language. Half Moon has a foul tongue on him. You wouldn't believe it."

I smiled apologetically. "I'll watch what I say."

Papa pointed a finger the size of a Mars bar. "You better, kiddo. There's a lady in this house, you know."

I almost asked *who*, but remembered Genie just in time.

"Sorry."

Papa spun a file along the kitchen table.

"One left. All the rest are accounted for."

I was flabbergasted. "One? You cleared the entire month of September in ten minutes?"

Papa shrugged. "No court would convict, but they did the deeds, all right. This other one is a new player."

I opened the first file and read the single typed page.

Incident Report
Subject: Isobel French (details below)
  Miss Isobel French is a dance teacher from
the town of Lock. On the evening of August
eighteenth, at approximately eight PM, Miss

French was returning home after a dance class in the community center. As per usual she had her personal CD player in her bag for the walk home. When Miss French put on her headphones and switched on the music, her head was immediately filled with noise of an unusually high volume. Miss French describes the sound as "like feedback, only a million times louder." The sound was sufficiently loud to partially deafen Miss French for three days. Her sense of balance has also been disrupted. Miss French's doctor advised her never to wear a personal CD player again, and to avoid loud noises for a period of eight weeks.

Miss French decided to sue the manufacturers, and took her CD player to an engineer. The engineer discovered that the headphones had been tampered with. The volume inhibitor had been removed and powerful micro speakers had been added. He concluded that person or persons unknown must have taken Miss French's headphones and replaced them with this extremely dangerous pair. It was at this point, 5 September, that Miss French and her father, Mr. Frank French, reported the incident to the police.

I closed the file. A dancer unable to dance. The victim was older, true, but it was the same man, I could feel it. Our mysterious giant. But even though I knew this, it brought me no closer to him. He was out there, somewhere close, manipulating our lives with his unfathomable crimes.

I looked up. Red and Papa were looking back at me.

"What?"

Red patted my shoulder sympathetically. "You were talking to yourself, Half Wit, sorry, Half Moon."

"I was not."

Red allowed his eyes to glaze over. "It's the same man. I can feel it."

Papa's shadow fell over me. "You said something about a giant, too."

I thought fast. "It's a quote from Arthur Conan Doyle. A metaphor for our problem."

Papa squinted down from a great height. "So there's no real giant?"

"No. This is some kid picking on smaller kids. A smart bully, that's all. When we find out who it is, we ring the police. End of story."

Papa folded his arms across his chest "Because I don't want you boys putting yourself in harm's way. Red can handle himself, but you, Half Moon, would be knocked over by a gentle breeze."

Red hustled me out of the kitchen. "Harm's way," he scoffed quite convincingly. "Don't worry about us, Papa. We're not tackling anyone. As soon as Half Moon charts this new file, then he finds the connection and we're on the blower to the police. Then he's out of your hair and everything's back to normal."

"Back to normal," sighed Papa wistfully. "I like the sound of that."

Back down to the bedroom.

Red propelled me inside. "Okay. You've got everything you asked for. The files are sorted, you visited a couple of crime scenes, and you have your computer. So how long will you need, half an hour?"

I got the feeling I was beginning to outstay my welcome.

"Red. It's not that easy. We're not connecting the dots here."

"Well, you better do something, Half Moon, because I don't have a single clue what to do. Not one. If you can't find something in those files, we're up the creek."

"Don't worry," I said. "We're not sunk yet. I have a few ideas."

Red ballooned his cheeks, blowing out a breath. "Good. I was beginning to worry that you weren't as smart as you're always saying you are."

I shot Red with two finger guns. "Hey, don't worry about it."

"I thought we talked about the finger gun thing."

"Sorry."

"I'll give you an hour then. I know you brainy types like to be alone."

"Appreciate it."

The door closed and I was alone. Alone with my ideas, of which there were exactly none.

Alone in a strange room. With strange people outside the door. With Lock's police force outside the walls. The future was bright.

I stood in that room, dizzy with failure. Everything I had learned had brought me to this moment, and now I felt useless. The badge in my pocket was just a lump of metal. It meant nothing if I couldn't solve this mystery.

I had a bunch of files. Crimes that had been committed against the youth of Lock. The youth. That was the only connection, but it wasn't enough. There were too many young people in Lock to check them all. Some of the victims were in the same school. Saint Jerome's. But not all. Most were teenagers, but now Isobel French, in her twenties, came dancing along.

What else? There must be something else?

I wasn't tall. I wasn't cool. I couldn't play sports. Being a detective was all I could do. All that made me different. I had to find a connection.

What was it?

I scanned over the files again. Running my fingers under each line. Checking birth dates. Addresses. Star signs. Anything. But I was wasting my time. It was impossible to group all the victims in one bunch. It was useless. I was useless.

Bernstein says: *Sometimes you know things that you don't know you know. Trust your subconscious. Let your instinct guide you.*

This had always sounded a bit "Use the Force" for me, but I was desperate. Maybe my subconscious already knew what was happening here. All I had to do was let the knowledge flow through me. Somehow.

Count Albert Renard, the famous French criminologist, used several exercises to free his subconscious. One involved a map and a set of darts. When he couldn't figure out where his prey was hiding, he would blindfold himself and throw a dart at a map of Paris. Very often the dart led the gendarmes to the correct address. Renard reasoned that his subconscious had already figured out the problem, and he didn't have the time to wait for his consciousness to catch up.

Could this technique work on photographs?

I printed off letter-sized prints of the file photos and tacked them to the wall. The closest thing to a dart in the room was a school compass in my pencil case.

This is ridiculous, I told myself as I pulled a pillowcase over my head. It can't possibly work.

I stood six feet from the pictures, peeking out from under the pillowcase until I had my general bearings.

Please don't let Red come in now. Please.

I dropped the pillowcase over my face. All I could see was a pale disk of light from the bulb and the crisscross pattern of the cotton case.

I stood there for a minute, trying to summon my

inner thoughts or my instincts or whatever, then pulled my arm back and fired. The compass bounced off the wall and whizzed past my ear. What was my subconscious trying to tell me? *Give it up, you fool, before you lobotomize yourself.*

I persevered, throwing the compass half a dozen more times until finally I scored a hit. The compass stuck deep, and was still quivering when I pulled off the pillowcase. The point was buried in April's photo. It had amazingly missed April and May in the photo's foreground and lodged in the forehead of a small girl by the school door. Another one of the victims. Mercedes Sharp.

"Ooh," I winced, plucking out the missile. Lucky it was only a photograph. "Sorry about that."

I examined the girl with the hole in her forehead. She was smiling, but it wasn't the typical girl smile. There was something mean in the way those teeth were clenched.

You're imagining it, I told myself. Seeing what you want to see.

I hurried back to the computer, using Photoshop to crop the picture until only Mercedes remained. She didn't look so pretty, wearing a sneer. Her hair was jet-black and pigtailed, and she wore a belted blazer over her uniform.

Was there something about this photo? Or was this a monumental waste of time?

I poured over the picture looking for some

clue. Any clue. Mercedes wore patent leather shoes, and a corduroy book bag slung diagonally across her chest. A single white headphone earpiece trailed from under the book bag's flap.

Something. Give me something. Maybe I should throw the compass again. Keep throwing until there was more hole than paper.

"So," said Red's voice behind me. "Is this our giant?"

Red was back. My time was up. Nothing to do but admit defeat.

"Actually . . ."

Red leaned in over my shoulder. "Mercedes," he sighed. "She's pretty as they come, Half Moon. But not someone to tangle with."

"Really?" I said, stalling.

"Roddy says she's actually a terror behind all the pink business. She squealed on Roddy's friend Ernie. He was expelled."

Curiosity straightened my spine. "Expelled? For what?"

"Mercedes saw him selling an iPod that he'd stolen from one of her friends." He shook his head. "Little Ern was always a bit light-fingered, although usually he stuck to sweets or cash to buy sweets. From iPod to cash to sweets would usually be one conversion too many for Ernie."

Something invisible tapped on my skull. *Helloooo, you're missing something.*

"An iPod? When?"

"Last week of school this summer. Don't you remember?"

I did remember. Last week of school. Just about the time this fun day photo had been taken. Ernie Boyle. Expelled for theft. Not his first offense, either. I had a file on him.

I looked at the photo again. There it was. Snaking from Mercedes Sharp's book bag: a white earphone on a white cable. Just like an iPod cable.

"Red," I said. "We need to talk to this boy Ernie."

"No time like the present," said Red. "We just need to stop off at the candy store first."

We tracked Ernie Boyle to a video arcade downtown. His mother was only too happy to tell us Ernie would be there, and offered us a fiver to bring him home. We turned down the contract. We had enough on our plate.

Ernie was the only kid in the arcade that afternoon, because everyone else was in school. Everyone except the suspended kid and the fugitive from justice kid. Ernie stood on a stool by the pool table, hustling strangers for candy money.

He was just finishing off his latest victim when we arrived. "Black in the center pocket," he said, then added insult to injury by not even looking at the shot as he played it. The black ball thunked down without so much as a rattle.

The loser threw a euro coin on the table, then walked out in disgust.

"There's one born every day," snickered Ernie, collecting his winnings. With his vest and cap, Ernie looked like he'd just escaped from a Dickens novel.

Red stepped into the glow of the table's strip light.

"Still hustling the hustlers, Ernie."

Ernie pocketed his winnings. "Well, if it isn't Red Sharkey. How's the assault-with-a-deadly-weapon business these days?"

Red picked up a cue. "Pretty good. I'm thinking of getting into it full-time."

Ernie backed down immediately. After all, he had a long way to go before he reached five feet, and even a six-footer would think twice before baiting a cue-wielding Red Sharkey.

"Just kidding, Red. Pulling your leg. Got any bull's-eyes?"

Ernie was addicted to bull's-eyes. They said his own mother wouldn't recognize him without a bulge in his cheek. This accounted for his smile being yellow, and black around the edges.

"I might have. What are they worth to you?"

Ernie twirled his own sawn-off cue like a baton. "Play you for 'em."

"No, no," said Red. "We want information."

"So all I have to do is tell you things, and you'll give me candy?" said Ernie suspiciously.

"Exactly. All we want is a sentence or two."

"Swear?"

"Swear?"

"Brick miss must celt?"

This was an Irish marble oath. If a kid took this oath and went against it, then he was branded untrustworthy for life.

"Brick miss must celt," intoned Red solemnly, performing the complicated hand routine that went with the oath.

Ernie grinned, and he really shouldn't have.

"Excellent. They don't sell bull's-eyes here, and I'm running low."

We squeaked into a leatherette booth.

"Now what can I do for you two Sharkeys?"

I looked around for the other Sharkey, then realized it was me.

Red nodded my way. "This is Watson, my cousin. He'll take it from here."

I cleared my throat. "I wonder, Ernie, if you could give us your own personal account of the day of your expulsion."

Ernie glared at Red. "He don't sound like a Sharkey, he sounds like law enforcement."

My cover was falling apart. I had to become a Sharkey. And fast.

I smashed my fist on the table. "Call me law enforcement one more time, and you'll be picking those bull's-eyes out of your ears!"

Ernie relaxed. "Sorry—no offense. What do you want to know?"

"The iPod. Did you steal it?"

"'Course not. Not my style. They never found it, either. Little Miss Perfect points the finger, and they all believe it. It's a tragedy of justice."

"Travesty."

"That too."

Red took out the bag of candy we had stopped off for. He rolled a single bull's-eye across the table. "Yeah but, Ernie, you're always crying *It wasn't me*. How can we believe you?"

Earnest tucked the sweet into his cheek. "I don't care what you believe, Red. It's the truth. I wouldn't know what to do with that pod thing. I just take candy or cola. Stuff like that. Stereos are more my brother's area. *Les Jeunes Etudiantes* had it in for me, so I had to go."

I wrote that down. "They had it in for you? Why?"

"I dunno. Their head honcho, Devereux, cornered me in the yard one day, going on about how boys are ruining their education and how it's got to stop."

This didn't sound like the *Jeunes Etudiantes* I knew. April and co. were more interested in pop stars than pop quizzes.

"Ruining their education? How?"

Ernie tapped the table. Red rolled another

164

bull's-eye across. It disappeared just as quickly as the first one.

"Me and the boys would be having some fun, you know, hiding the teacher's books, setting the paper basket on fire. Harmless fun, and April says we're interfering with their lessons. Can you believe that?"

I tried to appear sympathetic. "The nerve." A good investigator gains the interviewee's trust however he can.

"Yeah, one day, after I've superglued the teacher's desk closed, April Devereux gives me this piece of paper. There's nothing on it, and she says that's what's in my future if I don't stop disrupting the class. She says it's a warning. The next week an iPod goes missing and Mercedes swears she saw me selling it at the school gate. I offer to turn out my pockets, and there's twenty euros in there. I dunno how it got there. Honest."

I closed my notebook. It was a solid lead, if it was true.

"This is a solid lead, if it's the truth," I said to Red.

Red passed the rest of the candy to Ernie, who crammed at least six of them into his mouth.

"Ernie, you know me. You know my family."

"Mmhuh," said Ernie.

"I believe what you say. I'm going to act on this information. If it turns out to be a pack of lies, Roddy is coming over here for a chat."

Ernie stopped chewing. The bull's-eyes collected in his mouth like ball bearings in a vase.

"Ish the trush. *Brick mish musht cell.*"

Red was satisfied. A sportsman like Ernie would never break the marble code.

10

THE YOUNG STUDENTS

IT WAS BEGINNING TO LOOK as though my employer had more to do with events than she let on. I decided to pay her house a visit, except this time she wouldn't know I was coming. But first, Red and I headed back to Chez Sharkey to pick up a few tools of the trade.

When we arrived at the house, Herod was seated at the kitchen table sifting through a pile made up of two BMW wing mirrors, a digital TV dish, a trawler's global positioning box, and six Bob the Builder videos.

He glanced up at us. "Look at this. Fifty smackers' worth right here. People just leave this stuff lying around."

Red rattled the digital dish. "Bolted to their roof is hardly lying around, is it, Roddy?"

Herod grabbed the dish. "What do you care? I'm just doing what Sharkeys do. I don't think you're a Sharkey at all. I think you must be adopted. Last week I even saw you reading that horse book, *Black Beauty*."

"You did not," protested Red. "Well, so what if you did. Reading is better than robbing!"

Red pointed to the stash. "This has all got to go back."

"In your dreams. Who are you going to tell? Your new best friend? Half Moon, here? Or his best friend, Sergeant Hourihan?"

"It's your funeral," sighed Red. "I'll write to you in prison. Unfortunately you won't be able to read it." He nodded at me. "Come on, Half Moon, let's not waste any more time here."

"That's right, Red," taunted Herod. "Off you go with your bestest buddy, Mr. Nerd. The two nerds together. You two are made for each other. You should get engaged."

We put up with this abuse for as long as it took to devour a bowl of homemade soup and pick up Red's surveillance equipment bag. It didn't seem to bother anyone that two young boys were heading off with a sackful of spying gear. I know my Dad would have wanted an explanation for every item in the bag, but then the Sharkeys were not a normal family.

Whatever normal was. I wasn't exactly normal myself. My own dad had told me so.

We came and went by the back door, as there was still a policeman posted out front. Red was in foul humor all of a sudden. He cycled like a robot, his legs pumping the pedals tirelessly. His shoulders were hunched to his ears as he hauled on the handlebars for more leverage. He spoke not a word.

I was getting used to being the passenger, rolling into the corners with the bike.

We crested Coalyard Hill and freewheeled down the other side. Red gave his legs a rest and leaned back against me.

He grunted half in apology, half in annoyance.

I managed to stay on the bike. "Are you all right, Red? What's bothering you?"

Red didn't say anything for a long time, so long that I thought he had forgotten the question.

"You saw Roddy back there," he said suddenly.

My brain had moved on to the case, and it took me a moment to remember what I had asked.

"That's what's bothering you? Herod and his stash?"

"He's ten years old. And already he's stealing the school blind. Mom didn't want that to happen. Before she died, Mom asked me to watch out for my baby brother. I was only small myself, but I promised. I'm not doing a great job of it. I try to keep him on the straight and narrow, but I can't even keep myself out of trouble. It's like destiny or something. I can't escape the life that's waiting for me. Dad's life. Genie's life. Roddy's, too."

I didn't know what to say.

"You can give Herod a good example," I ventured. "Give him someone new to look up to."

"You think so?"

"Why not? Maybe he can be a detective when he grows up?"

Red chuckled. "Detective Herod Sharkey. Now that would be something. Criminals beware."

"You're not his dad, Red. You can't be. If you're going to keep Herod out of trouble, then you need Papa's help. Does he know about this promise you made?"

"No. Believe it or not, you're the only one who knows. I don't know how Papa would cope knowing Mom asked me to look out for Herod."

"You need to tell him. As soon as you can. Tonight."

Nothing for a while. Then, "Thanks, Half Moon."

April Devereux's house wasn't actually a castle, but it was supposed to look like one. The rear was adorned with stone cladding, vaulted arches, stain glass windows, a mini-turret, even a *Romeo and Juliet* balcony. April's bedroom was inside the balcony. Two marble unicorns guarded her window. April was standing between them, waving down at the group of girls being dropped off. Land Rovers and BMWs scored long arcs in the gravel and swung back out between slate-gray pillars.

"Looks like *Les Jeunes Etudiantes* are having a sleepover," said Red, peering through the railings.

We stashed the bike behind a hedgerow, then scaled a massive oak tree inside the walls. Red climbed like a monkey, seeming almost weightless. I, too, climbed like a monkey. A very old one with one leg and six fingers. I am not very nimble at the best of times, and my sore arm and swollen head slowed me even more than my natural inability. When I eventually scaled the trunk, we set ourselves up on a fork.

Even from that distance we could hear squeals and chattering from the hallway. The girls huddled and bounced, delighted to be together on a school night. They waved good-bye to their parents, then filed upstairs to the unicorn room.

Red pulled a pair of binoculars from his backpack and followed the dozen or so girls.

"Lotta pink," he commented. "Somewhere pink sheep are freezing to death."

That was a pretty good private eye–type comment. Red was coming along.

"Can you hear anything?"

Red glanced sideways for a moment. "These are binoculars, Half Moon. They only work on eyes."

It occurred to me that private eye–type comments could be really annoying after a while.

I held on to a branch, leaning out until my elbow creaked. "I can't hear anything. We need to get closer."

Red rummaged in his backpack. "I have some audio surveillance equipment."

He tossed me a Soldier Sam toy walkie-talkie. "Audio surveillance equipment? We're supposed to be professionals."

"It's got a range of ten feet, and six Soldier Sam phrases in Soldier Sam's actual voice."

I pretended to be impressed. "Ten feet? Wow. That's nearly as far as I can hear."

Red snatched the radio, stuffing it into his sack. "I think you're forgetting who the cool one is here, and who is the escaped criminal nerd on the verge of getting a thump."

I had a flashback to the sports pitch, when Red had jammed his hurl under my chin. That seemed a lifetime away, and this was a different Red. But you never know. . . .

"Point taken, but we still need to get closer."

Red hopped down from his perch, landing on his toes and the fingertips of one hand. I hopped down, too, landing on my face and one cheek of my bottom. Which is not easy.

"Come on," hissed Red.

"Arrumf," I replied.

We crept across the Devereuxs' garden. It was dark now, but the pink glow from the unicorn bedroom cast a fake sunset across the pale gravel.

"I feel like we're breaking into Disneyland," muttered Red.

I didn't comment. I was too nervous. This casual spying might be tame stuff for a Sharkey, but it was still pretty new to me.

April's parents had thoughtfully planted a stout creeper below the balcony, so Red didn't even have to use the grapple hook in his bag to get us onto the balcony. He was a bit disappointed about that.

"I shouldn't have packed this," he whispered, as we sneaked onto the balcony. "You know how heavy it is? You can carry it back."

I barely noticed what he was saying. I had wriggled to the glass door. The strange ritual being enacted inside made me forget my nerves completely.

"Get over here, Red," I whispered. "You have got to see this."

The Unicorn Room was like something out of a macho man's worst nightmare. Pink everywhere. Doors, lamp shades, drapes, duvet covers. All pink. Every shade from pastel to neon. I could feel my eyeballs sizzle just looking at the walls.

Red joined me at the glass door. "Wow. As I said, lotta pink."

Les Jeunes Etudiantes were gathered around a puffy fringed footstool. Pink. April Devereux stood on the footstool, arms outstretched like a preacher. The dozen or so other girls listened raptly to every word she said, and listening raptly is very unusual for ten-year-olds, especially in a large group.

"We need to hear what she's saying," I whispered.

"No problem," said Red, activating one of the Soldier Sam walkie-talkies.

He tugged at the bottom corner of the French door, and it opened a crack. Unlocked. Red pulled slowly, until there was a big enough gap to wiggle his arm through. Not one of the girls noticed, too busy preaching or being preached at.

"Now for the hard part," said Red. "Be ready to jump if this goes wrong."

Before I had a chance to object to that ludicrous statement, Red tossed the walkie-talkie across the room. It landed on the bed, nestling between a fuzzy bunny and a heart pillow. Both pink.

Red winked. "Impressed?"

I winked back. "I'll be even more impressed when you get it back."

Sometimes it's nice to be the brains in the group.

"How's the behind, Half Moon?" said Red, not as lost for words as I'd hoped. "I bet you'll have a nice bruise in the morning."

Time to change the subject. "We're on surveillance here, Red. We can insult each other later."

Red twisted the volume wheel on the second walkie-talkie. The first unit was set to broadcast, so we could pick up every word spoken inside. We lay flat on our stomachs, our jaws dropping wider as events unfolded in the Unicorn Room.

April Devereux was dressed and adorned from head to toe in pink, from her Barbie PJ's to the fluffy beret to the pink strands braided into her hair.

"Greetings, sisters," she said. Her voice sounded different. It was thin but fierce.

"Greetings, Mademoiselle President," responded her girls, all in their pink PJ's.

Mademoiselle President? These girls were taking their little club a bit seriously, weren't they?

"Why have we gathered today, sisters?"

"To solve the problem of the ages, Mademoiselle President," intoned the girls. Their tone was muted, but their eyes were bright and excited.

"And what is the problem of the ages?"

It was a one-word answer. "Boys!"

April Devereux punched the air with tiny clenched fists.

"Yes. Boys. For too long boys and grown-up boys have ruled this earth and made a mess of politics and ozone and stuff. For too long us girls have been not listened to by males, even our dads and brothers and people who should know better. How do we change this, sisters?"

"By ruling the world," chanted *Les Jeunes Etudiantes*.

"Exactly. Correct. You are spot on, my sisters, so smart. We will be prime ministers and managing directors and partners in law firms and owners of music stores that ban heavy metal and stuff with skulls. But for now, what are we?"

"Students."

"Correct. We are *Les Jeunes Etudiantes*. The Young Students. And this is how we must change the world. From our desks. From the classroom. What is our duty?"

The answer came promptly. "To learn."

"And what is our goal?"

"Knowledge."

Red elbowed me in the ribs. "This girl is a nutcase, but she's hardly a giant."

I hissed at him to be quiet, from the side of my mouth. There was something unique and sinister going on here, and I didn't want to miss a second of it. There was far more to April Devereux and *Les Jeunes Etudiantes* than they revealed to the world in general. April's little speech didn't sound very *pink*.

"The only way to power is through knowing stuff," continued the high priestess of weird. "But the old enemy stands in our way."

The other girls actually hissed.

"Boys. Horrible, smelly, big-mouth boys."

More hissing from the floor. Red and I were starting to feel unwelcome, though no one knew we were there.

"Ever since kindergarten, boys have been grabbing all the attention with their shouting and fighting and rude noises. How are we supposed to learn with all this going on?"

The sisters clapped and squealed their agreement.

"Aaron, for instance. Picking his nose all day. I don't know where he puts that stuff, but it's not in a tissue."

Much groaning and wincing in the audience, and outside the window, too.

"And Gerry, with his insects. How many of us have found something disgusting in our *petit filous*, thanks to Gerry."

Several hands went up. Apparently Gerry had been a busy boy.

"And I hardly need remind you of Raymond."

"RAAAYMOND!" They howled his name like a dirge.

"That boy is thicker than a milk shake," lamented April. "All day wasting teacher's valuable time with his dopey questions. 'What color is a smell?' 'Which way is up when you're asleep?' 'Does a basketball live in a basket?'"

There were cries of *Moron*!

And one, unexpected. "I like Raymond. He does nice pictures."

April groaned. "May. I know you don't bother coming to most of the meetings because of your

177

precious dancing classes, but now that you're here, try to keep up. You don't like Raymond. Remember, I told you. He's nasty and horrible. Remember how he smells after curry day?"

May giggled. "That's just being a boy."

There's always one missing the point. "Being a boy is bad, May. We don't have to put up with boy stuff. We need to take charge. Be the bosses like we should be."

May nodded, but you could see she was doing it to be in the gang.

"So you hate boys?" April prompted.

"Yep. Well, sometimes."

"May?"

"Hate 'em. Hate 'em. Can't stand 'em."

"Better." April clasped her hands. "Now, girls, I mean, sisters . . ."

"You're my cousin, April, not my sister," said May.

"May!" screeched April, pointing a stiff finger. "Shut up! You're ruining the meeting. We're not real sisters. Just pretend. It's a game. If you can't play along, you'll have to go home."

May chewed her lip. "Sorry, April. But I can't go home. Dad says we have to play together 'cause we're cousins. Dad says I'm supposed to ignore you if you start acting like a snotty princess."

April almost launched herself off the footstool; only the presence of the other girls stopped her.

She was the president and must act accordingly. April took a deep breath, sucking it down to her toes.

"Now, girls. It is time for our transformation."

Les Jeunes Etudiantes lined up excitedly in two rows before a poster of the pop star Shona Biederbeck in a dance pose. Shona was the undisputed princess of pink. A girly icon with a squeaky voice and several platinum CDs under her sequinned belt.

"What do people see when they look at us?" asked April.

"They see little girls," answered the little girls.

"And what do they think of us?"

"Sugar and spice and everything nice."

"And what do they not see?"

"*Les Jeunes Etudiantes*," chorused the girls.

"And why do we use the French words?"

"Because boys are too stupid to understand English, not to mention French."

"Now the moment has come for us to show our true selves. Our secret selves. Sisters, you may transform."

"Trans . . . what?"

"Change, May, change."

"Okay. Sorry."

The girls pulled off their pink pajamas to reveal dark pantsuits underneath. Pink scrunchies were replaced with black butterfly clips. Pink slippers were kicked off and leather shoes slipped on. April ceremoniously snapped off ten false nails, and pulled the pink strands from her hair. The final touch came when she turned her fluffy beret inside out. It was black on the inside.

She pointed at the poster of Shona Biederbeck. "Whose dream is this?

"A boy's dream."

"Is it ours?"

One voice. "Yes."

"May! Be quiet. Is this our dream?"

"No!"

"Well then, sisters. What is our dream?"

April jumped from her podium and tore the pop princess's poster from the wall. Underneath was a picture of Mary Robinson, the first female president of Ireland.

"Hail to Mary," said April.

"Hail to Mary," repeated *Les Jeunes Etudiantes*.

"This is our dream. We want to be just like Mary Robinson. We can grow up to rule the country."

"Whoopee!" screamed the other girls.

April winced. "I've been thinking about that. Whoopee is a bit too *Shona* for me."

"It's on her second CD," said May, starting to sing. "Whoopee, look at me."

April plowed on. "So instead of whoopee, could we say *Wonderful*? Or *Affirmative*? I saw that on *Star Trek*."

"On the one where the thing's head explodes?"

"No, May. On the one where they couldn't find enough stuff to power the thing."

"I loved that one."

"Me, too. At least we can agree on something. Now to business."

April pulled a clipboard from behind her headboard.

"Last year there were a few boys giving us trouble. So we made a list."

Outside on the balcony, I remembered that I should be writing all this down.

"With a little help from *Les Jeunes Etudiantes*, four of those boys decided to move to other schools, two learned to keep their big mouths shut. And three would not take a hint, so we had to have them expelled. Most recently, the iPod plan."

The girls applauded politely.

April laughed modestly. "*Merci, merci*. It was nothing. I think Master Ernie Boyle learned his lesson."

I gasped. A confession. I couldn't believe it. We had actually come to the right place.

"But there are still a few more to go. The first on our list is a boy so gross, so stinky that he makes Ernie look like, well, a girl. I think we all know who I'm talking about."

They knew, all right, and so did Red. I heard him groan and saw his shoulders slump.

"Master Herod Sharkey!"

Herod. Of course. These girls would hate Herod.

"Roddy, you idiot," muttered Red. "You've actually driven these girls crazy."

April flicked over to a page dedicated to Roddy's activities.

"Last year Master Sharkey wasn't much of an interruption, as he spent most of his time at home *sick*."

The girls nodded knowingly. Obviously Herod had been cutting class. Even ten-year-olds knew it.

"But this year he has been in for four days, and in that time he has hit two students, one in the stomach. He stole all the teacher's chalk and ate it. I know it was him because he stuck his tongue out at me. He didn't do any of his homework, not so much as a single math problem, which is a terrible example for the other poor boys who are easily led, on account of them being thick."

"Herod can stand on his hands," said May, a witness for the defense.

"That's all very well, May, but he shouldn't be doing it on his desk. No, he has to go. We can't take any chances with our education. We start long division this year, and that's hard enough without Master *Handstand* Sharkey interrupting every two minutes."

Another girl piped up. "Let's plant some money on him. Then say we saw him selling something."

"Very good, Amanda, but we did that already with Ernie. We have to try something new. I have an idea. Mercedes will you join me?"

Mercedes stepped smartly through the ranks.

"Show the sisters your arm."

"Yes, Mademoiselle President."

Mercedes rolled up her right sleeve, revealing a mass of purple bruising.

"Look at this," said April shrilly. "Herod Sharkey did this."

May was horrified. "Really? Herod did that?"

"Of course not, May. Don't be soft. Mercedes's pony threw her this afternoon, but we don't want Bouffy to get in trouble, so we're blaming Herod."

Outside on the balcony, Red tapped my shoulder. "Are you getting this?"

I tapped the pad with my pen. "Every word."

"So the Soldier Sam walkie-talkie was a good idea?"

"I suppose," I admitted grudgingly.

Inside, April was explaining her plan. "Tomorrow, I'll bring poor, scared Mercedes to see Mrs. Quinn, and she'll explain how Herod twisted her arm but she was too scared to tell."

"I've learned my part," said Mercedes proudly. "Just like in drama class."

"Would everyone like to hear Mercedes's speech?"

A chorus of *Yes, please.*

Mercedes smiled brightly, climbing onto the footstool.

"Okay," she said, shaking her fingers. "This is a

drama exercise to get yourself in the mood. Everyone shake their fingers, as though they're hot sausages and you're trying to cool them down."

Soon there was enough finger-shaking to cause a breeze. I only noticed that I was shaking too, when Red slapped my hand.

"You're supposed to be writing."

"Sorry."

"As you're shaking," continued Mercedes from her little stage. "Say: 'Shake shake shake silly supper sausages.' That's a vocal exercise."

"Obviously we won't be doing this tomorrow," said April, a bit miffed at losing the limelight. "Okay, I'll be Principal Quinn, you be you."

April folded her arms and deepened her voice. "Now, Mercedes, what seems to be the problem?"

Mercedes stopped shaking. "Just a sec, I have to find the well of my emotions." She stared off into the distance, until her eyes teared up.

"Oh, that's very good," said May.

"Thanks. I'm thinking about my puppy that got eaten by a wolf."

May was horrified. "Your puppy was eaten by a wolf?"

Mercedes rolled her bleary eyes. "Of course not, silly, I'm an actress. Now, Mademoiselle President, I'm ready."

"Are you sure? We won't have time for all this tomorrow."

"I'm sure. Quick, before I remember that I never had a puppy."

"Now, Mercedes," said April a touch grumpily. "What seems to be the problem?"

"Oh, Principal," gushed Mercedes. "I can't tell. My good and responsible friend April made me come here. But *he* will kill me if I tell."

"Who will kill you?"

"Herod Sharkey . . . Oh, no, I've said his name! He'll know. That boy is the devil."

April placed her hands on her hips. "I might have known. Herod Sharkey. What has he done now?"

"Please, Principal Quinn. You're a woman. You understand how it is in this man's world. We suffer in silence."

"Not in my school, young lady. Now, tell me what Herod did. Tell me this instant!"

Mercedes, dramatically and with much wincing, revealed the bruises on her arm.

"He gave me a skin burn, Principal Quinn. *He* thinks it's funny."

"Well, I never," said April/Principal Quinn. "This is disgraceful. I will expel him immediately. Blah, blah, blah. Herod is history, another victory for *Les Jeunes Etudiantes*."

Mercedes bowed modestly to an enthusiastic round of applause.

"We have tried to remove Herod before, but his

brother Red seems to always show up in the nick of time. Like a redheaded guardian angel."

May snorted with laughter. "Good one. Red-headed guardian angel. I'll have to tell Red that."

"That is not a joke, May. Red has destroyed my plans more than once. But not this time."

"Because of Bouffy's hair," said Mercedes, who couldn't bear to give up the spotlight.

April took a laminated curl of hair from her pocket. "Yes, Bouffy kindly donated this lock of fake Shona's hair, which I had planned to plant in Red's gear bag, but Red got himself suspended all on his own, and by the time he comes back it will be too late for little Herod. We will have washed our hands of him."

More applause. While they were clapping, I caught up with my note taking.

"'Herod is history,'" I muttered. "'Another victory for *Les Jeunes Etudiantes*.' This is dynamite."

Red clapped me on the back. "We've got to get this to your friend Murt. One look at Queen April's clipboard should put us both in the clear."

I was certain of it. My gut told me that *Les Jeunes Etudiantes'* various activities would tie in with our own crime list, but nothing was concrete yet. I would have to give Murt a few hours to match the crimes to the criminals. Anyway, maybe April would make it easier on us and confess to a few more stunts.

But at that moment the batteries ran low in the

second Soldier Sam unit. The one *inside* the Unicorn Room.

"More power," said the walkie-talkie. "Soldier Sam needs more power, soldier."

"Oops," said Red. "I think we're busted."

April Devereux tracked the noise like a cat tracks the squeak of a wounded mouse. She pounced on the walkie-talkie. She stared at it for a moment, wondering how it had got on to her bed. What was it doing there?

I scrambled to my feet. That girl was smarter than I had thought. She would figure it out.

Sure enough, the truth dawned on April. "Someone's listening!" she screeched. "Someone is spying on us, sisters!"

This was too much for Red. He clapped his hands and squealed in fake falsetto. "Someone is spying on us, sisters!"

"There!" shouted April, pointing. "On the balcony! Boys!"

"Boys!" they howled the word like banshees from the darkest corners of limbo.

"That doesn't sound very friendly," said Red, glancing back at me. I swear he was grinning. Grinning! "Come on, Half Moon, cheer up, they're only little girls."

Only little girls, true. But I saw under the crook of my arm that April was handing out junior golf clubs like rifles from a rack.

Her voice crackled with static over the dying speaker.

"Get them. They're burglars, so it's okay to hurt them as long as it's accidental."

Hurt us? Who were these girls?

"Come on, Red. We need to go. If we get into a fight with a group of ten-year-old girls outside their bedroom, we're going to look like the bad guys."

Red's chuckles rattled to a stop like a faulty motor. He knew exactly how the police would see this: Red Sharkey casing another house to break in to. Social services would have him in a home faster than you could recite *Les Jeunes Etudiantes'* credo.

Red grabbed a unicorn horn, swinging up onto the railing. "Okay. We go. But we're not running away, we're . . ."

"Making a tactical retreat," I offered.

"A tactical retreat," muttered Red, followed by a groan.

The French doors opened behind us. Girls poured out like beetles from a crack in the wall. Their clubs were raised and their eyes were bright.

April spearheaded the attack. I noticed for the first time that she had all her grown-up teeth, and they seemed really big in that tiny mouth. Especially when she was snarling.

"Come on!" shouted Red, grabbing my collar.

April's club swished as she swung. It was a putter. Graphite shaft. Amazing what you notice. That steel head could do some real damage to a person's head.

Fortunately the putter missed my head but did whack me on the shoulder, giving me a dead arm.

"Ow!" I shouted. "Hey. Watch it."

"They're just flesh and bone!" shrieked April triumphantly.

This can't be happening. This can't be real.

Then Red had me by the collar, swinging me out over the balcony, into space.

"Grab the ivy," he grunted.

I reached for the creeper with my good hand. I had it, too, in my grasp. We could have escaped—then I heard two things. A metallic twang, like you get when you bang a taut steel cable with a stick. And Red's voice saying softly "Oh, no."

Neither of these sounds was encouraging.

Suddenly Red was not holding us up anymore. We fell, fast and hard. There wasn't time for my life to flash before me. My shoulder scraped the wall, I saw the moon, then I was up to my ears in gravel.

Not too bad, I thought. Then Red landed on top of me. I felt like a cartoon character who had just been hit by an anvil.

I didn't lose consciousness altogether, but I lost the ability to do anything. Things happened around me that I could not connect with. It was like watching a movie from inside a fish tank.

There were girls, and gravel crunching and whispering.

"Alive. They're alive."

"Shut up, May. Daddy will hear."

"Should we . . ."

"No, Mercedes. No need for that. Grab their ankles."

"That's Red Sharkey. They're both Sharkeys."

"How much did they hear?"

"Doesn't matter. Who's going to believe dirty smelly Sharkeys?"

I was lying on a beach in the surf, with the undertow dragging me across the pebbles. Maybe. That's how it felt. My shirt rode up and stones gathered between my shoulder blades. My head flopped sideways, and Red was inches away. His face was covered in red. His whole face.

THE POWER OF MAGNETISM

I KNEW I WAS UNDERGROUND before my eyes confirmed it. Something about the deadness of the air. I was lying on a stone floor, a tiny stream of water pooling at my cheek. A dozen skinny-girl legs swayed in my vision, like reeds on a riverbank.

"What now?" said a voice.

They were still talking. Why couldn't they shut up? I had a headache.

"We can't wait until morning, sisters. I'll have to go now. To Principal Quinn's house. Daddy will take me. He does whatever I say."

"But what about those boys? Red is hurt."

"May. I don't think you understand what *Les Jeunes Etudiantes* are all about. We hate boys.

Especially Sharkeys. Especially, especially burglar Sharkeys. Dad will find these two down here tomorrow and the police can take them away. They're going to prison eventually anyway. We're just like, accelerating the process."

"But. He's bleeding. . . ."

"I wonder if I could divorce you, May. Can you divorce cousins?"

The girls left, moving up cement steps through a square of moonlight. A wooden door banged into the space, and a bolt rasped across. I was left in total darkness, which was good. I needed a snooze. I turned my face to the tiny stream on the floor and had a little drink. Cool. A bit gritty, but fine. Now, to sleep.

Something about what happened nagged at me, keeping me awake. April knew who I was. She had seen through my disguise before, so why pretend now that I was a Sharkey? The answer came quickly, even through the fog surrounding my brain. Nobody cared what happened to Sharkeys. *Nobody would argue with her plan to lock two Sharkeys in a cellar.*

"Aaah!" said a voice. "My head is on fire."

I opened one eye. Red's head was floating in the blackness. A disembodied head with blood dripping from the chin.

"Red?" I said. "Where's your body?"

The head chuckled, then winced. Ghostly fingers touched a cut on a ghostly head.

"I really gave myself a whack."

I noticed a flashlight under the spirit's head. Then the rest of Red's body swam into my vision.

"You're not a ghost," I said, relieved.

Red beamed the flashlight along the wall until he found a light switch.

"You better get a grip, Half Moon," he said, flicking the switch. What seemed to be a blinding glare filled the room. It eventually settled to a watery forty-watt glow. "You heard what they said. We need to get out of here before they get to Mrs. Quinn's, or Roddy is up the creek."

I squeezed my head until the stars disappeared. "Who's up the creek?"

"Roddy! Roddy. Keep up, Half Moon."

My vision was clearing up a bit. "Reddy, Roddy, there's only one letter in the difference. That's confusing when a person is possibly concussed."

Red ignored me, shining the flashlight into his backpack.

"You brought a flashlight?"

"And antiseptic wipes," said Red, mopping his forehead with one. "We're on stakeout, remember?"

"Technically we're not on stakeout anymore," I pointed out. "*Technically* we're being held prisoner by a bunch of ten-year-old girls."

"No one must ever know about this," said Red, who looked a lot better now that his face wasn't completely covered with blood. "I have a reputation to consider. If word gets out that I'd been locked up by a shower of fifth-grade girls, every hard man looking to make a name for himself will come gunning for me."

I took a look around. We were in a coal cellar constructed from steel and concrete. It had probably once been an oil tank, but April's father had converted it. The cellar's rear wall was piled high with coal nuggets, and thick black dust floated through the pale yellow air. There was one wooden door. And it was, of course, locked.

Red checked his cell phone for bars. "No reception in here. We have to get out."

He tried the caveman method, battering the door with his palm and shoulder. The door didn't open, but the banging did disturb more coal dust and set sonic waves of hollow booming echoing around the chamber. Just what we needed.

The booming subsided, and we were left with the sound of Red panting.

"Less of the panting," I said. "This place could be airtight."

I scanned the walls and roof. There was no way to break out, unless Red had a police battering ram hidden in his magic backpack.

Red kicked the door a few times. More dust and still no open door. I coughed loudly to highlight the dust problem.

"Red, that's not doing us one bit of good, you know."

Red whirled. His features were wild. I had never

seen him this manic before, not even when he had me pinned to the ground.

"I have to get out," he hissed through clenched teeth. Sweat was running down his face, washing away coal dust and blood. "Roddy needs me. I promised Mom I'd look out for him. If he gets kicked out of school, he'll end up in the pool hall with Ernie." Red crossed the bunker in two bounds. "You're the brains. Think of something."

Red's eyes were veined from dust and possibly tears.

"Okay. I'll try. What do you have in the bag?"

Red emptied the backpack's contents onto the concrete.

"A couple of cereal bars, my ski mask, and a pair of tights. I lost the grapple hook."

I had to ask. "Tights?"

"You know, for over your head. In case you needed a disguise."

"Oh. I think I'm disguised enough, actually. With the hair and the earring and the tattoo." I spotted something on the floor. "What's that?"

Red picked up an iron spike. "It's a horn from one of the unicorns on the balcony. It snapped off. That's why we fell. So I suppose your man on the balcony is technically a horse now."

The horn was a foot long, and tapered to a dangerous spike. Steel painted dark green.

"A pity it isn't magnetic," I said.

"Why?"

"Well, if it were magnetic, then we might be able to draw back the bolt on the outside of the door. Possibly. In theory."

Red handed me the spike. "Can you turn it into a magnet?"

"Well, in a laboratory I could place it inside a magnetic field, or pass a current through it, then the horn would become magnetic."

I said this very confidently, as there was no chance that we could actually do it. In fact, all I knew about magnets for sure was that you could drag iron filings around a sheet of paper with them.

Red grew immediately excited. "We *can* pass a current through it."

I paled under my coating of coal dust. "What?"

"The lightbulb. All we need to do is pull out the wires."

That sounded extremely dangerous. We were more likely to send the horn ricocheting around the cellar than turn it into a magnet.

"I don't know, Red. I'm not sure about polarity and all that stuff."

"We have to try something, Half Moon. I promised Mom. Don't you understand? I promised."

I couldn't even begin to imagine what a promise like that meant. But it obviously had a strong hold on Red.

"Okay. But don't touch the actual wires and don't

let them touch each other. That much I do know for sure."

Red switched off the light and handed the flashlight to me. He then yanked the supply cable from the clips attaching it to the wall and ceiling.

"Okay," he said, holding the cable away from his body. "What next?"

I trained the flashlight on him. "Well, in theory, maybe, I turn on the switch, then you zap the bar. That should do it. If I were you, I wouldn't stand in front of the pointy end of that horn. You never know where the electrical charge will send it."

"*You* could zap it," suggested Red.

"True," I admitted. "But we'd have to wait a couple of weeks while I worked up the nerve."

Red took a deep breath. "Okay. Zap time. Just touch it?"

"Yes. I think. I'm no expert. But there may be some jittering."

"Jittering? What do you mean?"

"You know, when the power flows into the horn. Try to hold it steady."

Red swallowed. He was nervous, but determined. "Okay. Flick the switch when I give you the sign."

"What sign?"

Red took a moment out from being nervous to deliver a withering comment. "Oh, I don't know. I'll say something like *flick the switch*."

"Right. I'll see if I can remember that."

Red knelt beside the spike, making sure the copper wiring inside the cable had firm contact with the metal horn. "Right, Half Moon. Flick the switch!"

Every muscle and tendon in my body was tense. My shoulders hunched and my eyes squinted. My toes and fingers locked, and all the injuries of the past few days returned to chip away at the pain centers of my brain.

I flicked the switch. And nothing happened. Red might as well have been rubbing the horn with a twig.

"Is that it?" he asked.

"Eh . . . Keep it there for a minute."

I walked over to him. "Did you hear that?"

"Sorry, I was nervous."

"No. Not that. Do you hear a buzzing sound?"

Red leaned closer to the unicorn's horn. "Maybe. I think it's just the wire scratching the metal. My hand is shaking a bit. But don't . . ."

"I know. Don't tell anyone."

Red threw down the cable. "So is this magnetized now?"

I studied the horn in the torch light. It looked exactly the same.

"I dunno. Give it a try."

"And I won't get a shock?"

"Allegedly not," I said, covering myself against a possible lawsuit.

Red poked the horn with a single finger. "It's a bit warm, I think."

He fluttered his fingers over the metal, then grasped it gingerly. "No shock. Let's test it."

Red hefted the spike and crossed to the door. "Shine the light here, Half Moon," he said.

I shone the beam on the door. There was a damp line across the center.

"That must be where the bolt is," I said. "Water gets trapped behind it and seeps through over the years."

"Oh, the brains," said Red, insincerely, I suspect.

He placed the fat end of the horn against the watermark's edge, and drew it slowly to the left.

"Try it," he ordered, stepping back.

I pushed. No joy.

"No joy," I said.

Red swore. Then. "Stupid, stupid idea. Making magnets. We need something else, Half Moon."

"There is nothing else, Red. Try again."

Muttering choice phrases, Red did so, and miraculously, amazingly, unbelievably, on the other side of the door, the bolt started to scrape back.

"Slow, now, slow. Don't lose it."

"What are you? An expert? Do this every day, do you?"

"Just go slow. Shut up for once."

It occurred to me then that I had just told a Sharkey holding a spike to shut up.

"Your negative energy is interfering with magnetic flow," I said pathetically.

"*Grrr,*" said Red. Growling was not good, but it was better than pounding. He went slowly, drawing the bolt back inch by inch. We could hear it scraping along the outside of the door, like a metal thing scraping along a wooden thing.

Finally there was a clunk, and the door sagged a fraction.

"Open," said Red. "I'm finding this difficult to believe."

We pushed open the door, and there was May, with one hand on the bolt.

"April is crazy," she said simply. "So I snuck back to let you out."

I squinted at her. "Did you pull back that bolt yourself, or did an invisible force help you?"

May looked at me in a way that made me realize how stupid that question sounded.

"I pulled it back," she said. "Maybe April is right after all. Maybe all boys are stupid and smelly. You look terrible, by the way. Your head is too big for your body. I know another boy like that."

I grabbed the horn. "I have a big head because of all the brains in there. I magnetized this horn, didn't I?"

May took the horn and placed it against the cellar's metal wall. It didn't stick, not even for a second.

Clang.

"Possibly, I should have tried that," I said,

mortified to be outthought by a ten-year-old.

May turned to Red, who was obviously the sane one.

"You and your partner better hurry if you want to save Herod. April has talked her dad into going over to Principal Quinn's. They're on the way right now."

Red was off like a greyhound after a rabbit.

"Thanks," I muttered. "And keep an open mind on the magnetism thing. You never know, it might have been a factor."

I ran after Red, May's mocking laughter ringing in my ears.

Mrs. Quinn lived in a town house near Lock's railway station. She came from a long line of teachers, but was the first in her family to have reached the exalted status of headmistress. Mrs. Quinn credited this to her people skills, no-nonsense approach to discipline, and having the local chief inspector for a husband.

By the time Red and I arrived on the bike, the Devereux four-wheel drive was already parked in the driveway. Even worse, there was a police car parked in front of it.

Red skidded to a halt, resting his elbows on the handlebars. "Too late," he said between puffs. "Mrs. Quinn has already called in the cavalry."

I agreed. "I'm sure April's father insisted on it. Herod is being accused of assault."

We stashed the bike behind a neighbor's wall and crept around the back, where Mrs. Quinn was entertaining her guests on the patio. At least we could hear what was being said. We crawled across the garden on our bellies, hiding below the lip of the deck. I raised my head just enough to spy on the proceedings through the fence uprights.

April, Mercedes, Mr. Devereux, and Sergeant Murt Hourihan were seated around a pine patio table. Mrs. Quinn was pouring tumblers of cloudy lemonade. April and Mercedes were back in pink mode.

"I asked the girls to wait until you arrived, Sergeant," said Mrs. Quinn. "This is a serious matter. Mr. Devereux thought we needed police presence and Francis is away at a conference. How do you like the lemonade?"

Murt had been trying to avoid drinking what was in his tumbler. He took a swig, and coughed most of it back into the glass.

"*Aagh, hurup,*" he spluttered. "God, that tastes like . . . I mean, oh, that went down the wrong way. Lovely, a bit tart, but lovely. Thanks."

Mrs. Quinn swilled the mixture around in the base of the jug. There were lumps floating in the hazy liquid.

"Another drop, Sergeant?"

"Ah, no. I'm on duty. Anyway, I have a code forty-three dash seven waiting for me in the station, so if we could get on . . ."

I happened to know that a forty-three dash seven was a maternity leave request form.

"Of course, Sergeant. Criminals never sleep, eh? Well, you know Mr. Devereux?"

"Evening, sir."

"Sergeant."

"Mr. Devereux brought the girls over. It seems they were afraid to come to me at school, in case Roddy Sharkey would see them."

"Red?"

"No, his brother Roddy. Herod, if you can believe it."

Murt took out his notebook. "Oh, I can believe just about anything of Master Herod Sharkey. We've had words."

"His mind is already made up," whispered Red. "We have to go in there. Give ourselves up, tell Hourihan what really happened."

I tugged Red's sleeve. "Wait. That won't help anyone."

Red shrugged me off. "Maybe not. But I have to try. I promised."

"One minute," I said desperately. "Give me a minute. If I don't come up with something, then we'll go in."

Red settled back down reluctantly. "One minute. And I hope this plan is better than the magnetism one."

I had a feeling that I would be hearing about the

magnetized unicorn's horn for quite some time.

I returned my attention to the patio. April was giving Murt the big round angel eyes.

"Mercedes was crying at our sleepover, Sergeant. It was pink night. We're all in pink, because that's what girls do, and we're just like any other girls."

Murt cleared his throat. "Pink night? Is that why I came over here? I have better things to be doing. I promised Art Fowler I'd check his vending warehouse for that prowler that's been spotted. So I do have somewhere to go tonight."

"Ah now, Sergeant," objected Mr. Devereux. "Be patient. They're only kids."

Murt had heard too many sob stories to be a soft touch. "I'm a busy man, sir. Let's hear what the girls have to say, and see what has to be done about it. April?"

"Well, it's not me, really. It's Mercedes who has the problem. I'll let her tell you. Mercedes?"

Mercedes stood, walking with slow deliberate steps to a better vantage point. She cleared her throat and flicked her hair. Preparing herself to repeat the performance we had seen in the Unicorn Room.

The performance!

I pulled my notebook out, flipping to my Unicorn Room notes. I had written down Mercedes's entire routine.

I scrawled a cell phone number on the notebook,

then passed it to Red. "Text this page to that number. Quickly."

"Why am I . . ."

"Quickly," I hissed. "No time."

Mercedes was shaking out her fingers. "Shake shake shake silly supper sausages," she said automatically.

This surprised the adults somewhat.

"Excuse me?" said Murt.

"She's nervous," said April hurriedly. "And upset, too. Isn't that right?"

"Yes," agreed Mercedes, with tears in her eyes. "My puppy got eaten by a wolf."

Murt rolled his eyes. "Right, I'm off. Thanks for the wild goose chase, Mrs. Quinn."

"No, Sergeant. I'm ready now. Please."

"One more chance. And I don't want to hear the words *pink*, *sausages*, or *wolf*."

Mercedes took a deep breath to speak, and Murt's phone beeped.

"That was quick," I said, startled.

"First sentence only," said Red, without looking up from his screen. "I'm going to send it in bursts."

Murt took out his phone. "Keep going there, Mercedes. I'm a trained professional; I can read texts and listen to sausage stories at the same time."

"Oh, Principal," gushed Mercedes. "I can't tell. My good and responsible friend April made me come here. But *he* will kill me if I tell."

"I suppose you mean Herod Sharkey?" said Mrs. Quinn, straying from the script.

Murt was absently reading his text message, when Mercedes's words penetrated. He suddenly sat bolt upright in his chair.

"What did you just say?" said the policeman, then caught himself. "Nothing. Go on, keep going."

Mercedes dragged at her cheeks, leaving red finger marks. "Herod Sharkey . . . Oh, no, I've said his name! He'll know. That boy is the devil."

"I know who it is, Mercedes. You told me that already."

Murt opened another text. Mercedes continued with the prepared monologue. "Please, Principal Quinn. You're a woman. You understand how it is in this man's world. We suffer in silence."

Mrs. Quinn was confused. "What are you talking about, girl? We suffer in silence?"

Mercedes, dramatically, and again with much wincing, revealed the bruises on her arm.

"He gave me a skin burn, Principal Quinn. *He* thinks it's funny."

There were tears rolling down Mercedes's cheeks as she said this, but Murt was not impressed, as he was reading the exact same words on his screen. This was obviously an act.

He nailed Mercedes with his best bad-cop stare. "What is going on here? One chance. Start talking."

Mr. Devereux rose to his feet, knocking a glass of

congealing lemonade. "Sergeant Hourihan. How dare you talk to this poor girl in that tone!"

"I dare, sir," retorted Murt, very theatrically, "because this girl is reading from a script. The same script that someone has just texted to me. Someone with my cell number . . ." Murt paused. He was no fool. "Someone who can't show himself for some reason." He looked around. "Someone who's running his own investigation."

Red and I ducked low, wriggling into the mud.

Mr. Devereux climbed up on his high horse. "Just what are you suggesting, Sergeant? You're not saying that somehow my little girl is involved in this deception?"

Murt's phone beeped a final time. "That's exactly what I'm saying, sir. And my source informs me that this isn't the first time. My text buddy advises me to take a look at April's clipboard, which is hidden behind the headboard of her bed."

"So now April is the ringleader? Ridiculous! You can search behind any headboard you like. Trust me, my little girl does not hide clipboards. She has no need to; we're a very open family."

Mercedes's lip was quivering. "Bouffy!" she blurted.

April pinched her friend's arm cruelly. "Quiet!"

"Bouffy threw me," sobbed Mercedes.

"You total idiot," snapped April. "You are soooo like a boy. They have nothing. Nothing!"

Mercedes was on a blubbery roll. "I didn't want

to do it. Mademoiselle President, I mean April, said we could get rid of Herod the way we got rid of Ernie and Jimín and Kamal. April said that Bouffy wouldn't get in trouble."

Murt was puzzled. "Who is this Bouffy person?"

"My pony. She threw me and I bruised my arm."

Now Mrs. Quinn was involved. "You got rid of Ernie? And Jimín?"

Mercedes folded completely. "April did it. She made us swear not to say anything. April made me take the iPod, and then she planted the money on Ernie."

"What about Jimín? You couldn't have done that. It was his voice on the school loudspeaker."

April couldn't resist explaining. "Jimín is so stupid he couldn't give you a rhyme for cat. We simply had him read a long passage into a computer microphone, then edited it down. He was happy to do it for a minute's attention."

Mrs. Quinn was looking less like a gracious host now, and more like an irate headmistress.

"And Kamal's little present on my doorstep?"

Mercedes blushed. "Bouffy did that."

April crossed her legs at the knee. "This is so frustrating." Her moment of anger was over, and now she had to talk her way out of this situation. "Surely you understand, Mrs. Quinn. I had to get rid of the boys; they were interfering with our education."

Mr. Devereux slumped against the wall. "Oh my God, my mother was right. She's become a spoiled monster." He straightened. "Right, young lady. This is the final straw. You are going to do whatever it takes to undo whatever it is that you have done."

April actually sneered. "Oh really, Daddy? Shouldn't you check with Mommy before handing out punishments?"

Murt slammed his palms on the table. "Quiet! All of you. It seems as though a crime has been committed here, so this is a police matter. I need to see that clipboard, Mr. Devereux. Any objections?"

April stuck out her lip. "You need to check with Mommy before answering."

"I do not need to check anything!" shouted her father. "You have my full permission to see whatever you like, Sergeant. No warrant necessary."

Murt pocketed his phone. "Excellent. I'll be around early tomorrow, about eight-thirty." He turned to Mrs. Quinn. "And if I were you, I'd be begging those boys you expelled to come back before their parents get themselves a lawyer."

April was dumbstruck. For about half a second.

"I just do not *believe* this," she shrieked. "You should be thanking me. You *should* be giving me a medal. I have made your jobs easier by a *million* percent."

Murt was not in the mood. "If I was you, missy, I'd shut my trap before my blood pressure gets any more elevated."

April paled, as though physically slapped. "Did

you hear that, Daddy? He told me to shut my trap. Are you going to let a mere sergeant speak to me that way? Don't you play golf with Chief Quinn?"

April's dad wagged a finger at Murt. "Really, Officer. She's just a child, a baby, really. I hardly think . . ." Then his resolve returned. He took a cell phone from his pocket, dialed a number, and waited.

"Hello, it's me," he said when the person on the other end picked up. "How would you like a visitor? Yes. What we talked about. I'd say a month. Oh, right away. The sooner the better."

Mr. Devereux pocketed his phone. "Right, missy," he said, trying for the same impatient tone that Murt had used. Trying but not succeeding. Mr. Devereux sounded a note below terrified. "After Sergeant Hourihan has finished with you, provided you are not in a jail cell somewhere . . ."

April cupped her mouth. "Hello, Earth calling Father," she said brazenly. "I'm a minor, remember?"

This latest insult gave April's dad courage. "Well, good, we won't have the jail problem, then. Which is just as well, because you'll be away. On a vacation. For a month."

April's brazen look fell away. "Where?"

Mr. Devereux squared his shoulders resolutely. "Your grandmother's."

April screamed long and shrill. "Granny's! The farm! But they give me chores! There's no TV or Internet!"

"Good," said Mr. Devereux, a bit shakily.

I felt the sooner April got on that bus the better, before her dad lost his resolve. "You don't mind if April misses some school, do you, Head-mistress?"

Mrs. Quinn seemed preoccupied. "Now I'll have to change those boys' pictures in their files. April's too. I had her down as a little angel, but that was all wrong. I've never had to change a picture before."

"I'll take that as a no."

Mercedes patted April's shoulder. "Don't worry. I'll chair the meetings. And I'll tape *Question Time* for you."

April slapped away her friend's hand.

"I am the president. Nobody chairs the meetings but me." She stood, straightening her pink corduroy skirt. "I'm just going to leave now. You grown-ups need a while to think about your decision."

Mr. Devereux's nostrils flared. "You are going nowhere. I'm putting my foot down this time."

April walked off the patio. "Of course you are, like the last million times."

"You get back here!" shouted Mr. Devereux, with a hint of desperation in his voice. "You are not in con-trol here, April!"

Murt was losing patience fast. "I have somewhere else to be, sir. So either you control your little girl, or I will."

The adults followed April around the side of the

house to where the cars were parked. Red and I crept out from behind the decking to watch the action.

April had climbed into the family car and locked the door behind her. Her little face was wrinkled with determined fury.

Her father rapped on the window. "Open the door, April. Right now!"

April wrapped her thin fingers around the wheel. "I'm going home, Daddy. You can come when you've calmed down."

This statement did nothing to calm *Daddy* down.

"You're what? In my car? You don't even know how to drive! I swear, if you put so much as a finger-print on my baby, you'll spend the next *year* at my mother's."

Obviously the car was Mr. Devereux's weak spot. April was not impressed.

"Oh, grow up, Daddy. It's just a hunk of metal."

"But you don't know how to drive!" shouted Mr. Devereux, the tendons taut in his neck.

"How hard can it be?" said April, turning the key, which her father had thoughtfully left in the ignition. "I've watched you a thousand times."

"April! Turn off the engine!"

Murt thought all of this was hilarious, until he noticed the squad car was directly in April's path.

"Now listen here, missy," he said sternly.

But April couldn't see or hear him. The engine noise smothered his words. April wrestled the automatic gear stick to DRIVE and let off the hand brake. Two seconds later, the Devereux four-wheel drive rolled into Murt's squad car at ten miles an hour. Plenty fast enough to do almost twelve thousand euros worth of damage.

April had just enough time to see the looks on the adults' faces before the air bag wrapped itself around her.

THE PROMISE

WE RETURNED TO Chez Sharkey flushed with victory. Though Red may have been flushed from carrying me on the back of his bike all day. Genie was at my computer again, downloading songs from an Internet pirate site.

"That's illegal," I said.

"So are you," she said. A good point.

"Where's Papa?" asked Red a little nervously. He had gotten himself all psyched up to talk about the promise he had made to his mother.

Genie slipped a recordable CD into the drive. "He's out. Working."

"Where?"

"I can't talk in front of the N-E-R-D."

I rolled my eyes. "I can spell, you know."

"Really? Then G-E-T L-O-S-T."

Red squeezed his head between Genie and the screen. "Where is he? I need to know."

Genie sighed. "Very well, my annoying little brother. He's at the vending machine warehouse. Papa's been scoping it for a few days now."

Vending. That was the second time I had heard that word recently. It was unusual to hear such an uncommon word twice. Murt had said it earlier tonight. He had promised to check the vending warehouse. Someone had been hanging around. A prowler. Murt could very well catch Papa in the act.

"We have to stop them." Should I have said that? Papa was committing a crime. I was on the side of law and order, wasn't I? But Red was my friend. And his family was in danger.

I tugged Red's sleeve. "We need to go now and stop him."

Genie folded her arms. "Here we go. Time for the piglet detective to deliver a lecture. The world is not black and white, Half Moon. Some of us do just fine in the gray areas."

"Murt Hourihan. *Sergeant* Murt Hourihan is on his way to check out the vending warehouse right now. Remember?"

Suddenly Red did remember. The memory turned him whiter than a nervous ghost. "We have to go," he said. "Right now."

The quickest route to the Lock Industrial Estate was cross country. We sprinted through several gardens and across a wasteland of discarded machine parts, heading for the orange glow of the estate's streetlamps. The farther we went, the farther Red pulled away from me. He was in good shape, a sportsman. Running flat out for a mile didn't seem to bother him. Me, I thought I was going to die. And after I died, possibly throw up. I didn't call Red back, though; speed was more important than brains in this instance.

The estate was U-shaped. Three rows of buildings with an entrance on to the main road. The entire place was lit up like a flying-saucer landing site. I imagine they would light those up pretty well. I saw Red tearing across a parking lot, surrounded by several of his own shadows.

By the time I caught up, he had located Papa behind the vending machine warehouse. He was wedged into a ditch overlooking the loading yard.

"Would you like to tell me why I shouldn't go in there?" Papa was saying. It was obvious that he was not happy with Red's sudden appearance. Then he noticed me.

"You brought Half Moon? On a job? I know you don't exactly think like the rest of us, Red, but you're still family."

Red's bottom lip jutted out. "You just can't go in there," he said stubbornly. "That's all."

Papa emerged from the bush. Quite a bit of it stayed in his hair. With the orange glow behind him, Papa looked like a caveman emerging from a hole in time.

"Listen, son. We all know how you feel. But I'm the way I am. Stop fighting it. Just accept it. Nothing's going to happen to me. I've never been caught. You know that. I'm too clever for the police."

"Can't we talk about this at home?" asked Red. "We need to go home."

"Why do we have to go home tonight?" asked Papa suspiciously. "You never came after me before."

I thought I would fill in the details. "Murt Hourihan is on his way. . . ."

That was as far as I got because Papa eyes were wide and his voice grew loud. "Murt Hourihan. Sergeant Hourihan? You've gone over to the other side, then, Red. Did you turn me in?"

Red rolled his eyes at me. *Well done, Half Moon*, said the eyes. "No. Of course not. I would never do that. We're here to save you." Red stood his ground. "Don't do it, Papa. Trust me. You go in there, and you're in prison and we're in care. Is that what you want? It's not what Mom wanted."

Papa was quietly furious. "That's it!" he said, pointing a finger bigger than a hot dog. "The line is crossed. Don't you throw your mother at me. You were barely five."

"I know what she wanted," insisted Red.

"You know nothing!" shouted Papa. "This is me, Red. In front of you. I am your family. Not our unwelcome guest. No offense, Half Moon."

"None taken," I mumbled.

"This is my life," said Papa, spreading his arms. "What do you want me to do about it?"

Red said nothing. He simply pointed toward the main road. A solitary pair of headlights bobbed through the darkness, then turned in to the industrial estate. The car materialized under the street-lamp glow. It was a squad car with a crumpled rear bumper. The car disappeared from view around the front of the warehouse. It did not reappear at the other side.

Papa stuffed a tool kit under his arm.

"Home," he ordered. "This conversation is not over."

Back to Chez Sharkey for the final time. There wasn't much said on the way. This would be my last night here, one way or the other. Even if we hadn't steered Murt to the clipboard, the twenty-four hours that Papa had given us to break the case were almost up. As it turned out, it hadn't even taken us that long.

The police watch hadn't stretched to another shift, so we were able to walk through the front yard. Red and I dawdled at the door, reluctant to face Papa again.

"I have to sort out this family thing," Red said. "It

could be loud, Half Moon. So why don't you go home now?"

I had asked myself that same question. I was desperate to see my parents and sister, but I needed to be strong for a few more hours. Until Murt had sewn it all up. It would be fascinating to see how it all tied together.

"Because it's not a hundred percent yet. It may take the night for Murt to trace everything we've been accused of back to April and her gang. I want all the loose ends tied up before I turn myself in."

Papa was waiting for us in the kitchen. The trip home had given him the opportunity to calm down, but he hadn't taken it.

"In here, the two of you," he roared.

We considered disobeying, but not for long.

Papa's eyes sparkled with annoyance from below brows that could have taken a few braids. All the man needed was a helmet with horns and he could have been a Viking.

"Right, Red. Start talking. What exactly is going on in that head of yours?"

"It doesn't have to be like this," Red whispered, his eyes on the floor. "You've made your choice, and so has Genie. But me and Roddy don't have to have the same life."

Herod laughed. "I want to do it. I have every video game in the charts in my bedroom. I don't need friends. I just need my console and a bag of candy!"

Papa was taken aback. "You have us, too, Roddy boy."

"For now," said Red, louder now. "Until you go to jail along with Arthur and Uncle Pete and Mad Mary and Eileen. There'll be a whole wing of Sharkeys soon. If it wasn't for Half Moon, you'd be in a cell right now."

Herod spoke quietly. "Are you going to jail, Papa? When?"

Papa frowned. "No, I'm not going to jail."

"Me neither," added Genie. "I'm too fashionable for those orange jumpsuits."

Red was determined to make his point. "Tell him the truth. Before you drag him into a life of robbing and thieving."

Papa was flabbergasted. I got the impression that this was the first time one of his children had ever pressed him on this subject. He recovered, and tried to joke his way out.

"Ah, now, Red boy," he sang, dancing his way past the kitchen table. "We're hardly master criminals, just shave a bit off here, skim a bit off there." He took Red in his arms, waltzing him around the kitchen. "Relax, little man. Aren't we happy? Don't we get along just fine?"

Genie and Herod were dancing, too.

Red broke away from his father. "Mom made me promise!" he cried, his eyes wide and rebellious. "I was only five, but Mom made me promise that

I'd keep an eye on Roddy. But how can I with the pair of you up to your armpits in every swindle going? What kind of example are you?"

This was family stuff. I should be elsewhere. Home with my own family, having our own fights. Suddenly I longed for some of Hazel's drama-queen hysterics. I would even wear whatever shirt Mom picked out for me. And Dad. Dad. Just thinking about them made my insides hurt. I wanted to throw up. Then sleep for a few days.

Papa had stopped dancing.

"You promised your mother? She asked you? Hardly more than a baby. Why not me?"

He already knew the answer, but Red told him anyway. "You'll never change. But there's still time for Roddy and me. We can be normal."

"I don't want to be normal!" stated Herod. "What am I going to do? Be a private eye, like you and your new best nerd friend?"

Red was upset now. "You're too young to know what you want!" He sat at the table, hiding his face in his hands.

Herod laughed. "Sure, have a little cry there, Mary. Should I get you a hanky?"

"Shut up, Roddy," snapped Genie. Her eyes were brimming with tears. "Why didn't you tell us this before?"

Red spoke between his fingers. "I was trying to keep an eye on the sly. Not turn everyone against me.

It's getting too much now. Herod is a one-man crime wave at school. The police are already watching him. For his sixteenth birthday he's going to get a set of handcuffs."

Genie took a tissue from her sleeve and wiped her eyes. "Papa, maybe Red is right."

Papa threw up his meaty arms. "Another one. Are you all against me?"

Genie stood her ground. "Don't take it personal. We're not against you. We're for Mom, and Roddy, too."

Papa's fingers disappeared inside his beard as he scratched his chin. "Well, maybe I could rein him in a bit."

"What?" yelped Herod. "You can't rein me in. Especially not because of Red."

Herod had forgotten that you don't give orders to Papa.

"I can't rein you in?" he thundered. "Can't? I am the master in this house. You will do as I say. From now on, school three days a week and no robbing."

"Three days a week!" howled Herod. "I'm not a robot!"

Papa's mind was made up. "Three days. That's it. Maybe four after Christmas!"

Herod ran to his room, howling like a wolverine. He did pause on the way past to punch me on the arm.

"I know this is your fault, Half Moon!" he said, before disappearing down the corridor.

Papa turned his gaze to me. "How long have you been hanging around?" he asked, as if all this family upheaval had been my fault.

"Just today."

"Seems longer. Anyway, your time is up in the morning."

"I know. Twenty-four hours."

"It's okay, Papa," said Red. "It's all over. We cracked the case. By morning we'll be in the clear, then he can go home and we can all get back to normal."

Papa nodded slowly. "All over? Wrapped up quick and easy. I have an instinct for crime. This isn't over. Nobody's going back to normal just yet."

Instincts versus facts. Papa had one, I had the other. I was right. This case was dead and buried. And there are only two ways something can come back from the dead. One, in dreams. And two, if someone has buried the wrong body.

I felt a twinge of doubt in my stomach.

"I need to go to my room," I said. "I have to check my notes."

My files were where I had left them, strewn across the furniture and floor. Generally when a case is wrapped up, hindsight makes it easy to connect the dots. When you know who dunnit and why they dunnit, how they dunnit is not so difficult.

So. April Devereux wants to get rid of the troublesome boys in her class. What does this have to do with May Devereux or Adrian McCoy or Isobel French or Maura Murnane? On the face of it, nothing. But there must be some method in her madness. Some ripple effect. It was impossible to know without that clipboard. Murt would figure it out. He would slot the pieces of the jigsaw into place, and I would be welcomed back into law-abiding society with bear hugs and sloppy kisses.

I lay on the bed among files and photos. The ancient mattress sagged alarmingly under my slight weight.

Mom, Dad, Hazel: Sorry. Home soon. Love, Fletcher Watson Sharkey Half Moon Moon.

I was getting all emotional—running through reunion scenarios in my head. An alarming number of them ended with me being grounded until I got married and moved out. You know you're in trouble when your own imagination starts punishing you.

What have Les Jeunes Etudiantes *got to do with you?*

It was an annoying question because I didn't have an answer for it. Why had April and her comrades targeted me? I couldn't trace it back. The more I thought about it, the more it seemed that there were two separate cases here. Was it just as Murt had said on that park bench a lifetime ago: *Sometimes when you can't find a pattern it's because there is more than one.* Two sets of criminals. *Les Jeunes Etudiantes* and the mystery giant. Could that be? Had I simply stumbled across April Devereux's grand plan by throwing a dart at a photograph?

No, I decided. Not possible. The town of Lock was simply not big enough to support two conspiracies. There must be connections running weblike between the victims. I would have to be patient. All would be clear in the morning, as the weather forecaster said to the public. Except for, those weather forecasters were always getting it wrong.

My body fell asleep because it was so utterly physically exhausted, but I swear my brain stayed awake all night worrying. What if we were wrong? What if our giant was still out there lurking in the bushes? Looking for the next victim on his list.

By 8:30 AM I was up and dressed, pacing the hall outside Red's room.

"Are you awake?" I shouted, rapping on the door.

Genie's voice wafted through the adjacent wall. "Shut up, Half Moon. It's the middle of the night."

Red appeared at the door, his red hair standing in pyramid spikes.

"I need your phone," I said, flapping my fingers. "Quick."

Red threw his cell at me. "You're calling home, right? To tell them you're on the way?"

"No. I need to talk to Murt."

Red snatched the phone away from me in mid-dial. "Are you mental? Never call a policeman in the morning. Don't you know anything?"

"I need to know if we're clear."

"Of course we're clear, Half Moon. April and her weirdo friends were behind everything."

"Maybe. But maybe not."

Red sighed. "You are so paranoid, Half Moon." He handed the phone back. "Go on, put yourself out of your misery."

I tapped in the number. Murt answered on the eighth ring.

"Sergeant Hourihan. Don't you know better than to ring a policeman in the morning, whoever you are?"

"Murt, it's Fletcher."

I could hear Murt breathing loudly through the earpiece. It sounded as though he were trying to calm himself.

"Fletcher Moon," he said at last. "You made a right monkey out of me, Fletcher, or should I say, Watson."

Murt had put two and two together, and a lot quicker than I thought he would.

"Cassidy told me about the new Sharkey. And April just confirmed my suspicions. I'm on my way over. Do yourself a favor: be there."

I had no time for this. "Am I clear for the arson?"

"Listen to me, Fletcher. Forget this tomfoolery. You're in enough trouble."

"Am I clear?" I shouted into the phone. "Did the clipboard clear Red and me?"

Silence for a moment, probably while Murt waited for the ringing in his ear to stop. "I think it's a crime to aurally assault a police officer. And in answer to your shouted question, no, the clipboard didn't mention you or your partner in crime. You still have a lot of questions to answer. I can't help you if you won't stay still to be helped."

My heart dropped to the seat of my pants. We weren't clear. Our giant was still at large.

"Sorry, Murt. I have to go. Give me twelve hours."

Murt laughed. "Twelve hours. You're funny, Fletcher. Really. We'll have a laugh about this when we meet. Of course, there'll be a sheet of Plexiglas between us."

"Sorry, Murt."

"Don't do it, Fletcher."

"I've got to go."

"Flet—"

I cut him off.

Red had picked up the gist of the conversation. "The police are still after us."

"Yes. Murt is on the way."

Red tried to smooth his hair. With mixed results. "Okay. We're really under pressure here, Half Moon. What have you got?"

The question hit me like a whack of a shovel.

"Nothing. I have nothing. I need more information."

Red pulled on a sweatshirt. "What kind of information?"

"Facts about the victims. I need to find another link."

Red checked up and down the corridor. "What if I knew somebody who could give you that information?"

"Let's go. Murt is on his way."

"What about breakfast?" moaned Red. "Breakfast is the most important meal of the day."

I zipped up my garish tracksuit top. "Well, either we skip it, or we have it in the cells."

A GIANT'S TRAIL

"WHERE ARE WE GOING, Red?" I asked, wind ballooning my cheeks. We were freewheeling down a road pockmarked with potholes.

"To kick-start this investigation," Red called over his shoulder. "If you want to know what's going on in this town, there's only one place to go."

"The police station?" I guessed.

Red laughed so much he missed a gear change. "The police station! Are you serious? No one tells the police anything. No, this is the opposite of the police station. This is where Papa gets all his facts. This place is off limits to civilians. Papa warned me not to bring you here. But, you know, we're partners."

Partners? This was news to me. But good news.

Red steered past Healy Hill toward the suburbs. Not the fashionable suburbs—the other ones.

Red parked outside a semidetached end house with a cctv camera mounted in a mesh box over the porch.

We were no sooner off the bike when three track-suited kids congregated around us.

"Hey, Red," one called, a skinny specimen with Celtic spirals shaved into his hair, and half a dozen rings dangling from one ear. "I'll look after the bike for a euro."

Red rounded on the boy. "If anything happens to my bike, I'm going to hold you responsible, Rasher."

Rasher. There's one in every town in Ireland.

"Hold me responsible all you like, your bike will still be in bits."

Red gripped Rasher's tracksuit by the waistband and jerked down sharply. The entire pull-away bottoms came off in his hands, exposing the unfortunate kid's knobby knees.

"You get these back when I come out. And if there's so much as a bird poop on the handlebars, I'll be wiping it off with your pants."

Rasher nodded, dragging his T-shirt down to his knees.

"No problem, Red, and no charge."

"There had better not be, Rasher, or you'll be feeling the breeze."

Effective tactics. If every young vandal was forced to do his rounds without pants on, the world would be a safer place.

Red pressed the intercom buzzer.

"Step onto the frame, please," said a voice through the speaker. There was a white square painted on the doorstep. I squeezed on beside Red.

"Oh, look who it is," said a female voice. "The fugitive himself."

Obviously the resident had penetrated my cunning disguise. Who was this person, and what did she know that we didn't?

We proceeded down an ordinary enough hallway into an extended sitting room. Inside this room, an elderly woman sat in the center of what could only be described as an information empire. Her steel-gray hair was drawn back into a tight bun. She wore a tweed trouser suit, and a there was a Bluetooth headset clipped over one ear.

"My God," I breathed.

The old lady had converted her lounge into a Situation room. Three plasma TVs were mounted on one wall, running CNN, Sky News, and the BBC. Another wall was lined with filing cabinets, these were divided into categories, including THIEVING, VANDALIZING, and EXTRA M.

"What's extra M?" I asked.

The lady swiveled on her chair to face me.

"Extramarital affairs, obviously. No one gets hugged or kissed in this town without me knowing about it. You'll be glad to know, young Moon, that your own parents are kissing nobody but each other. They're in the minority, I can tell you."

I was amazed. "How do you know about me? Who are you?"

The lady tapped a brass nameplate on her desk. It read DOMINIQUE KEHOE. "I know all about you, Fletcher Moon. We are two of a kind. I am Lock's only other accredited private detective."

"I've never heard about you."

Dominique smiled. "That is because I didn't want you to, but I have been looking forward to this meeting for some time, even though we don't work for the same side."

Another wall was covered with thumbtack-spiked maps. I recognized many of the crime scenes. Dominique had spotted many patterns that I could never have worked out, even with my computer.

"Very impressive," I said finally. "But these can't all be cases of yours, so why do you do it?"

Dominique stood. "Because information is power, Fletcher. Everyone needs information at some point in their lives, and generally I can supply what they need—for a price."

"Do you get this from a source in the police?"

The old woman laughed. "Who tells the police anything?"

I was skeptical. "How detailed can your reports be, without police input?"

Dominique did not answer immediately; instead she crossed to a cabinet and selected a rather hefty file. "December, five years ago. Fletcher Moon buys a crochet pattern book."

I grew suddenly nervous. "Wait a minute, Mrs. Kehoe. No need for an exposé."

She flicked over the page. "Fletcher Moon enters and wins the county crocheting prize under an assumed name. The prize is never collected. Video evidence is available on request."

My windpipe almost seized up. "Video evidence?"

"Always reconnoiter your surroundings, Fletcher. There are cameras everywhere. Your package arrived in a garish blue envelope. You were filmed posting this package in the town center."

I smiled weakly at Red. "It was a fad. I'm over it now."

Red laughed. "Crocheting? You know something, I'm not a bit surprised."

Dominique selected another file. "Fletcher is not the only one with secrets."

She flicked through the file. "Last September. Red Sharkey joins the local library."

"It's a lie!" blurted Red.

"Oh, really. I have your records right here. In December you checked out *Black Beauty* five times."

Red coughed to cover his blushes. "I like horses, big deal. Now let's get down to business, Dominique."

"That's more like it." Mrs. Kehoe smiled. "First we get the formalities out of the way."

"Formalities?" I asked.

Dominique opened an invoice template on her computer. "I'm only helping you at all because I know you're innocent. But I still want payment, young man."

"How do you know I'm innocent?"

"Red told me."

"You trust Red more than the police's mountain of evidence?"

"Of course. Red has been a reliable source of information for years," said Dominique. "But that doesn't mean I'm going to help out of the goodness of my heart."

Red pulled out a battered Gore-Tex wallet.

"Usual rates, Dominique?"

Dominique filled in the date and client sections. "Oh, no. This is a special case. Premium rates. Two hundred euros, and no guarantees."

Red started. "Two hundred? Our futures are on the line here."

Dominique shrugged. "My heart bleeds, Red. Two hundred. And don't bother with your Sharkey bartering. I'm too long in the tooth."

"All I have is eighty, and we cleaned out both of our bank accounts for that."

"I've got something for you, Mrs. Kehoe," I said. "Something in the way of a trade."

"Not interested," declared Dominique, tearing off an incoming fax. "I deal in cash only."

"You know the Lock police have a Web site."

Dominique's ears twitched. "What about it?"

"If a person had the password, that person would have a lot of information at his or her fingertips."

Dominique tried to play it cagey, but her interest leaked out through twitching fingers.

"And you have this password?"

"I do. It's valid for the moment, but it could change any second."

"I have broadband," said Dominique. "You can download a lot of information in a second."

"So you'll help us, then?"

Dominique returned to her desk and opened an Internet browser on the computer screen.

"Not so fast, Fletcher. I need to verify the information. What is the password?"

I gave it to her, along with the name, rank, and number. I prayed that Murt hadn't changed his password.

Dominique keyed it all in, and an entire police force's worth of information opened up before her. She instantly looked ten years younger.

"You have yourself a deal, Fletcher. I see years of fruitful cooperation ahead of us."

I didn't know about that. We were poles apart as

detectives. Dominique wanted power; I only wanted answers.

. I took my pad from my pocket. "I have a list of names here," I said, tearing off a page. "I need a connection."

Dominique studied the names briefly. "School?"

"That was my first thought, but it only links Red, May, Mercedes, and myself. We're in the same school. But not the rest."

Dominique sat at her desktop, typing in the names one by one. "I'm working on a database for the entire town. People are connected by family, occupation, and residence. Let's see what these names bring out."

Moments later the computer retrieved every occurrence of the eight names. Dominique switched on a DAT projector, casting the computer screen's contents onto a whiteboard.

She tossed me a whiteboard marker. "Show me what you're made of."

I stood before the board, staring at the names, willing something to jump out at me. There were twenty index cards displayed on the screen. Most names featured in two cards, some in three. Family, occupation, and residence. In no instance did the eight names all feature on the same card.

"This is it," I muttered to myself. "The answer is here somewhere."

I circled the victims, then joined them with

ragged lines. That didn't teach me anything except how high I could reach on the board.

"Four in the school. What about you other people. Where did you meet? Is this a wild goose chase?"

I tapped Maura Murnane. The chocoholic.

Behind me, Dominique sighed. "Her mother is a holy terror, but Maura is a lovely girl."

I turned sharply. "You know her?"

"She babysits my grandson. He dotes on her."

A piece of the jigsaw thunked into place. Something white flashed behind my eyes. This is the moment investigators live for. I took several deep breaths before talking.

"Does she babysit for many families?"

"Yes. Parents love her. I have her client list on file."

I didn't need to ask. Dominique was digging in a cabinet, caught up in the excitement.

"What is it?" asked Red.

I ignored him. I had to keep going.

Dominique handed me the list. I flattened it on the wall, scanning the names. "There," I shouted triumphantly. "James and Izzy Bannon. Their daughter Gretel is in third grade. Saint Jerome's."

The connection. It was the school after all. We just had to cast our net wider.

I scanned the remaining names with fresh, enthused eyes. "Isobel French."

The young dance teacher's name appeared on three cards. There were two entries under name. One current and one from when she went by her birth father's name.

I ran my finger across to Isobel's family card. The name on the card was Halpin.

I thumped the board. "French is her stepfather's name. She's a Halpin."

Red snapped his fingers. "SeeSaw Halpin is in fifth grade. She must be his sister."

"We just need one more."

One more. So close.

Dominique switched on a laser pointer on her key ring, highlighting Adrian's name.

"Is that Adrian McCoy? The DJ?"

I could hear something in her voice. Excitement. Maybe we weren't so different.

"Yes. What is it, Mrs. Kehoe?"

"Adrian does some volunteering at the community center."

I knew what was coming. I felt it with total certainty. The same certainty experienced by people who suddenly remember where they left a lost item.

"Two boys in his group, Johnny Riordan and Pierce Bent, are from . . ."

"Saint Jerome's," blurted Red. "I know them. They borrow Adrian's decks sometimes."

My forehead felt hot. It buzzed like a space heater. "That's everyone. We got them all."

"No. Not everyone," said Dominique. "Most people don't report nuisance crime. But I hear about it."

"Well?"

Dominique pointed to a pile of files in her in-tray. "Take your pick."

"Come on, Dominique. Does anything stand out?"

Dominique thought about it for a moment. "Just one. A strange case. Martina Lacey. Someone sent her a paint bomb, in a bunch of roses. Miss Lacey moved back to Dublin after the event. She was too shaken up to stay in Lock."

I found the relevant file on the table. There was a cell number listed.

I handed Dominique the file. "Would you?"

"Of course."

Dominique dialed the number on her desk phone, placing the call on speaker.

Martina Lacey's phone was switched on. She answered on the third ring.

"Yes?" Her tone was wary. Scared, almost.

"Martina, this is Detective Byrne here, from the Lock station. We heard about the flowers you received from a friend of yours. We'd like to take a look at your case and I wonder if you could help us out?"

Martina's breathing rasped over the speakers. "I'm finished with Lock. I've put all this behind me. I won't press charges even if you do find someone."

"Just one question," said Dominique soothingly, a professional. "Then we're out of your hair. We're just trying to tie a few cases together; we won't even need your testimony if it comes to that."

"One question?"

"Ten seconds of your time, then you know you've done your civic duty."

"Okay, Detective." Her voice was small, like a mouse. Being a victim could change people forever.

"My question is this, Martina. When you lived here, in Lock, did you have any contact with pupils from Saint Jerome's national school?"

Silence for a moment. Then: "I gave after-school tutoring in mathematics. Preparing students for their entrance exams. One of my girls was from Jerome's. Julie Kennedy. Her parents were very strict. They promised to ground her indefinitely unless her grades picked up. I hope she got a new tutor. Is that all you need?"

"Yes, thank you, Martina. You've been a great help."

Martina hung up first, and the tone droned over the speaker for several seconds before Dominique remembered to do likewise.

"That's it," I whispered. "No question. Saint Jerome's *is* the link."

Red stepped close to the whiteboard until his shadow blotted out the projected names. "Okay. But the link to what?"

I didn't know yet. "I need more detailed information on our new list."

Dominique Kehoe checked her files. "If you don't have more details, and I don't have them, then who on earth does?"

I had a sudden vision of knitted cardigans and grinning dogs.

"There is one person," I said, and my voice may have trembled slightly.

LARRY AND ADAM

I WAS ONE OF THE Sharkey family now, and it was more than skin deep. The Sharkey gene ran through my system like a virus. It bullied my other genes and sent them packing to the darkest corners of my personality. I found myself walking hard and talking tough. It felt good to be the outsider. My previous existence seemed monochrome. Now I was living life to the fullest, appreciating every moment outside the police station.

Red had loaded himself up with gear: bolt cutters, a length of rope, mini-tool kit, flashlight, and two single egg frying pans.

"Frying pans?"

Red grinned, offering me the choice of a pair of

tights or a tin of boot polish. "Trade secrets, Fletcher. Watch and learn."

I took the polish and smeared the viscous gunk across my cheeks, feeling it sink into my pores. It would take months to scrape off, and underneath it would be fake tan. I offered the tin to Red.

"In your dreams, Fletcher," he chuckled, rolling his trusty ski mask over his face.

Saint Jerome's seemed different at night. When darkness fell, the school was stripped of its daytime identity and became just another town building. Without murals and hopscotch grids and exuberant children swinging from its gates, the school could just as easily have been an office block, or a prison.

We were huddled behind the security fence, Red and I, building up to the big break-in.

Red hefted the frying pans. "I'm trying to get away from this kind of life, Half Moon," he said, looking like a black fish inside his ski mask.

"I know, Red, but we have to do this. Our giant is still out there."

"It's very early for breaking and entering. Papa says don't go in until the nightclubs are closed. You never know who'll be walking home."

"We can't wait. Someone could get hurt."

Red sighed. "I'm not used to worrying about people outside the family."

He passed the frying pans through the fence, then clambered over.

"Tell me what the pans are for?" I asked through the bars, hoping this was not a view I would soon be coming accustomed to.

Red grinned, his teeth shining from the blackness. "You just come in when you hear my whistle." Then he closed his mouth and disappeared.

I felt suddenly alone, mainly because I was suddenly alone. But it was more than that. I was about to cross the line between bold and bad. If I actually participated in a break-in, then my face would become another mug shot destined for a police file. There was nothing I could do about it now. I had to get into Saint Jerome's. I needed to make the final connection before someone else was hurt and my own life disappeared like a sail over the horizon.

I heard Larry and Adam growling. The noise rumbled across the yard like the revving of two sports cars. I thought it was the most frightening noise I had ever heard, until it was followed by the rapid clicking of their clawed paws on the pavement.

I stood, grabbing the bars and shaking them, as though I could dislodge the metal poles from their cement beds.

"Red!" I called, mindless of our supposed stealth. "Get out! They'll eat you alive, or kill you, then eat you."

Then I heard the whistle. Two short notes. Maybe that was my signal to come in, or maybe Red didn't want to die alone.

"Red?" I hissed into the blackness. "Are you alive? Can you talk? Do you need stitches?"

A set of teeth appeared before me. "Will you please shut up? You heard my whistle, didn't you? So come on."

I struggled over the fence, without arguing. Red had faced Larry and Adam, and survived. His hard-man status was assured for life.

I crossed the yard, using years of memory to guide me. Ahead I could hear Red's footfalls and a gristly, slurping noise. My imagination, fed on years of murder mystery novels, supplied gruesome explanations for these sounds. When I drew closer to the shadows around the main building, I saw that the slurping noises were in fact slurping, as Larry and Adam licked the grease from the frying pans.

Red knelt between the dogs, slowly tethering them both to the school oil tank. "Roddy knows every security dog in Lock. They love him. I think it's because he's a bit of a mutt himself. You show any dog in a five mile radius these frying pans and they roll over to get their bellies tickled."

"Very clever."

Red shrugged. "An old trick. We never wash those pans, in case a dog needs distracting."

My stomach wobbled. I distinctly remembered Genie serving up sausages from those pans. How many dogs had licked them before now? It was probably wiser not to ask.

We skirted the hopscotch squares, tiptoeing across to the office window. The blind wasn't drawn and an alarm sensor squatted buglike on the sill.

"That's it," I said, sighing a whoosh of relief. I couldn't help it. "We can't open the window."

Red placed his toolbox on the sill. "I don't want to open it," he said. "Opening it would set off the alarm."

If Red was stating the obvious just to make me feel like a moron, it was working.

He selected a flat chisel from the box, sliding it under the strip of rubber that held the glass in place. He patiently wiggled the chisel across the bottom of the window, up the side, across the top and back to the beginning, removing each length of rubber as he reached a corner.

"Knock, knock," said Red, rapping smartly on the center of the pane; it flexed, then toppled from the frame. He caught it, laying it carefully on the ground. "The sensor is only activated if the window opens. This way, I don't break the connection."

Another nugget of Sharkey wisdom. A hundred and one things you don't learn in school.

"I'll remember that."

Red paused, then dropped his head. "Don't remember it, Fletcher. When this is all over. Forget everything we've done. I'm going to try. I've been trying."

It was dark and Red was wearing a mask, but I

knew how his face would look. Pained. This break-in was costing him.

He took a breath, then vaulted through the window frame into the office shadows. I clambered after him, not quite as gracefully, but I managed to gain entry without jarring the frame.

Red switched on his pencil flashlight. "Now, what are we looking for?"

I felt my way across to the desk. This office was making me extremely nervous. The musky odor of two Dobermans still clung to the walls, and the wet-wool smell of Principal Quinn wafted from the chair like a ghost of her presence.

"This," I said, hauling her ledger from the drawer. "Principal Quinn keeps a unique record of every student's school activities. We should be able to spot the final connection from the pictures."

The book was covered with velour wallpaper, patterned with paisley swirls. I heaved open the cover with two hands, and it thumped onto the desk. Red pulled the blind and switched on the desk light.

"Quick as you can, Half Moon."

I barely noticed the nickname anymore. It was the least of my worries. To be honest, I liked it now. It was like a battle scar.

The pupils were recorded alphabetically, and by year of enrollment. I flipped the pages forward until I came to the names I was looking for.

"Well?" asked Red.

My pulse began to race. I had seen something. My eyes blurred with excitement and my hands shook. Of course. Of course. Idiot. Moron. Call yourself a detective.

"Shut up," I hissed at Red. An offense punishable by a severe Chinese burn not so long ago. "I'm thinking."

It was all there in the pictures. The dancer. The karaoke queen. The DJ's. But I needed to be sure. I flicked back the pages to fifth grade. There was SeeSaw with a little dancer drawn beside his name. Then third grade. There was Gretel Bannon. And after her name a scrawled recorder. She was a musician. I checked the rest of the names. My theory was sound.

"It's the talent show," I whispered, as though speaking aloud would break the spell, shatter my deductions. "You were all in last year's talent show. May and SeeSaw danced, Mercedes did the karaoke, Johnny and Pierce were DJ's. Julie Kennedy and Gretel Bannon were musicians. You did your Elvis bit."

"Bit?" said Red, miffed. "It was more than a bit. I've had offers. Anyway, you weren't in the talent show."

I closed the book. "Don't you see? We were a two for one. When my attacker got me and blamed you, I was off the case and you were suspended." I snatched the talent show lineup from Mrs. Quinn's notice board. "They're all out of the show except May, even though he burned her lucky costume. He's probably going to go after her again."

"He'd better hurry up," noted Red. "The talent show started twenty minutes ago."

My knees almost gave way, and my voice rose a panicky octave. "Tonight. It's on tonight?"

Talent shows were not the kind of thing I kept track of. Bernstein would be disappointed with his star pupil. A good investigator should keep abreast of everything.

"Yep. I was doing 'Love Me Tender' before you came along."

I rubbed my forehead, cobbling a plan together.

"You're still doing it. May is not safe. We have to get in there."

"How? I'm suspended from school."

"Technically this is an extracurricular event, not held on school property. Only the community center committee has the power to ban Elvis from the building."

We left the office the way we had found it, carefully replacing the pane and rubber. Five minutes after we'd gone over the fence, the only sign that we had ever been there was the confused blinking of Larry and Adam.

I SEE THINGS AS THEY REALLY ARE—FINALLY

NOTHING IS GUARANTEED to pack 'em in like a kids' show. The Lock Community Center was jammed with little stars and their extended families. Some of the performers had entourages that would put an A-list movie star to shame.

Cars were jammed in the parking lot so tightly that it seemed as though they had crashed. Body heat pulsed in waves through the hall's open windows.

Red had texted his backup singers, and they met us at the stage door in full sixties regalia. Luckily the costumes had already been prepared, so all the Sharkeys had to worry about were the hairdos.

Genie's hair was piled atop her head in a rock-hard beehive. She wore a spangled minidress with elbow-length gloves and heels so high they looked like little ski ramps. Herod was there, too, in black sunglasses and stick-on sideburns.

"You really look the part," I said, trying to be friendly.

Herod swiveled his hips and shot me with two finger guns. "Well, thank you very much."

"All you need to do is get me inside; after that, go on with your act as normal. I need to watch May, make sure nothing happens to her."

Red frowned. "I've been thinking about that, Half Moon—nothing really happened to May."

I knew what Red was thinking, and I wanted to nip it in the bud. "Her lucky dress was burned, Red. I call that something."

"All that did was buy her sympathy. She's still in the competition. And that dress never did bring her luck, did it?"

I put on my best aghast face, which is not easy underneath layers of fake tan and shoe polish.

"What are you saying, Red? That May did all this to win a competition? She sabotaged her friends and burned her own dress, all for a little trophy?"

"Maybe. How well do you know her?"

"Well enough. I study people, Red. That's what I do. She helped us, didn't she? She saved Herod."

Red stuck his chin out belligerently. "Yes, well

maybe you've been studying May a bit too hard. Maybe you're getting romantic ideas."

My cheeks burned hot enough to melt the shoe polish. "She's just a kid, for heaven's sake."

Red surprised himself, and me, by backing off. "All right, calm down. It's a possibility, that's all. You're supposed to look at every possibility. You told me that, Fletcher."

It was true. I had—quoting the Bernstein manual. But May being behind all this wasn't even a possibility, was it? And why not? Because I liked May? Because I trusted her? I dismissed the niggling doubts. I could think about this later, when May was safe. And had Red just called me Fletcher?

The Cork officer, John Cassidy, was plonked outside the stage door. Extra security because of the threat from deranged escapees. He sat on a bar stool, arms folded across his chest. His eyes were glazed with boredom, but he perked up when he saw Red approaching.

"Look who it is, Elvis and the freak show. You're suspended, Red. You've about as much chance of getting in here as an ax-wielding psychopath. And Murt is looking for you, by the way."

Red said nothing, simply handed Cassidy his cell phone. The officer placed the receiver to his ear, which is almost impossible not to do if someone hands you a phone.

"Hello?"

"Hello?" said a male voice. "Who is this?"

Cassidy stood. "This is Officer John Cassidy, who is this?"

"This is Brendan O' Kelly Riordan, the Sharkeys' lawyer. I believe you are denying my clients their constitutional rights by refusing them access to a public performance at which they are registered to perform."

Cassidy stiffened. "I have my orders."

"That's all very well, but your orders are invalid. If you persist in enforcing them, then you will be named in the lawsuit."

Cassidy's head snapped back a fraction. "Lawsuit."

"Of course, lawsuit. You are traumatizing my client. You are stunting his mental growth. You are fostering antisocial behavior. Just ask young Red how traumatized he is."

Officer Cassidy covered the mouthpiece with a hand. "Hey, Red. How traumatized are you?"

Red's face grew long and weary. "Very. About ten grand's worth, at a guess. Of course, if I cry in court, it could be twenty."

Cassidy tossed him the phone. "I need to go over there for a minute, because of a suspicious noise that I just heard. If someone were to sneak in while I'm away, it's hardly my fault, is it?"

Red pocketed the phone. "Hardly," he said, leading the way into the hall.

We filed past Officer Cassidy. On this occasion even Herod managed to keep his trap shut. Cassidy was on a hair trigger, and one smart remark could have the lot of us thrown out on our ears.

As I squeezed past his belly, Cassidy laid a hand on my shoulder. "Keep an eye out for Fletcher Moon, Watson. He's a psychopath, that one, mark my words."

"Don't worry, Officer," I said, scratching the stubble on my brow, to hide my face. "Eyes peeled. That's me."

I breathed a quiet sigh of relief as I sidled into the hall. Obviously Murt hadn't spread the word that Watson Sharkey was actually Fletcher Moon. Maybe he was giving me the benefit of the doubt, or maybe he wanted to catch me himself.

The Lock Community Center's backstage area was jammed with bodies. Officer Cassidy seemed to have let in more than he kept out. Proud mothers combed their daughters' hair, pushy dads glared at rival contestants, and wannabe pop stars swanned around as though they were already double platinum. I couldn't see May anywhere.

"Okay," I said, eyes darting like a nervous deer. "You guys get ready to go on. I'll look for May, to warn her."

"Or tip her off," mumbled Red.

I ignored the comment. I couldn't deal with the

possibility that May could be behind this. I liked her.

Emotion is the enemy of truth.

Bernstein again. But I couldn't peel off my feelings like a Band-Aid. I was a real person, not a collection of words on a page.

Genie tossed me one plastic shopping bag, and another to Red. "Put these costumes on. We're supposed to be performing."

I was about to object. There was no time for costumes, but I realized that I wouldn't be of any use to May if every adult in authority stopped me to ask what I was doing backstage.

We ducked behind a wishing well constructed from cardboard boxes. Red's costume was from Elvis's Vegas period: a white jumpsuit complete with silver cummerbund and cloak. My own clothes were from the movie *Jailhouse Rock* and consisted of a black canvas suit and striped shirt. They were tailored to fit Red, and so I had to turn up the legs and sleeves.

Red twirled the silk-lined cloak over his shoulders. "You look ridiculous," he smirked.

In spite of the situation, I couldn't hold back a smile. We were conspirators on an adventure. Life was dangerous; you took your smiles when you could. And they meant more when there could be a madman lurking around every corner.

I threw a punch at Red's shoulder. He allowed it to land, though he could have dodged it easily.

"You big bully, Half Moon. I'd have our lawyer on you, if we had one."

I wasn't a bit surprised to hear that there was no Sharkey family lawyer. "So who was that on the phone?"

"Papa. He does a great fancy accent, picked it up at university. He has a degree from Trinity in philosophy."

Now that *was* a surprise. I was learning fast not to underestimate the Sharkeys in any field.

"I'll meet you back here," I said. "After 'Love Me Tender'."

Red pulled the tape off of the stick-on sideburns and pasted them to his cheeks.

"Okay. Be careful. I know you think May is the victim, but in the movies it's always the last one you suspect."

"This is real life. And in real life, the most obvious suspect is usually guilty."

I hurried away before Red could point out that he and I were the most obvious suspects. I shouldered my way through throngs of people. Every one of them knew me, and most were on the lookout for me. But I held my head high, wearing my disguise confidently. I was a Sharkey now, and people may sneer behind my back, but no one would challenge me.

May was not making herself easy to find. I found magicians with half-dead pigeons stuffed in their vests, a country and western band shedding sequins from their vests with every step, and two jugglers who kept knocking each other over with bowling pins. But no Irish dancers.

I was beginning to despair, when I heard May's tap shoes banging out an irregular beat on the wooden floor. It had to be her. Nobody else could have that startling lack of rhythm.

I followed the noise. There she was, in the shadow of an enormous bunch of balloon grapes. She was dressed in a new black-and-silver dancing dress, her blond hair draped across her shoulders. A shaft of light from an overhead window caught her tiara and split into a thousand rainbows. I stopped dead. She looked perfect. Too perfect to ever commit a crime, however petty. Surely, there was something wrong.

I studied her face for a sign of malice, but there was nothing. Just a slight frustrated pout because her feet repeatedly refused to perform as commanded. Time and time again the click-kick eluded her. She scissored her legs well enough, but she could never click her heels on the way down.

Something stirred in the deep shadows by the wall. Something darker than the shadows themselves. I peered into the darkness, zoning out the surrounding confusion. Someone was there, dressed from head to toe in black, sliding along the wall toward May. They were approaching with curiously exaggerated movements. I couldn't think of an innocent explanation for this behavior. This person was obviously the criminal mastermind moving in on his final target.

My stomach lurched and my heart pumped as though a fist was tightening around it. My mouth automatically opened to call for Red, but I checked the impulse. There was no time. I would have to handle this myself. I was not an expert in the field of direct action, preferring to point my police contacts at the criminals, but there was no time for channels now. I had to move.

The figure glided closer to its target, its movements fluid yet angular. Bigger than me. Much bigger. But I wouldn't need to contain the suspect, just knock him to the ground. The dark figure raised its hands, curling its fingers into claws like a TV vampire.

Move! I told myself. Now or never.

I did move, as though in a daydream. My brain couldn't believe what my feet were doing. I had no idea how to attack someone. There was no chapter on this in the Bernstein manual. I simply barreled forward. To the casual observer my attack surely resembled a prolonged stumble.

I have read books about detectives tackling suspects. These fictional characters are always expert in several forms of martial art, having spent at least a decade training on a mountaintop in the Far East. I have had no such training. The biggest thing I had ever tackled was a jar of pickled onions that refused to be opened.

I decided to add some noise to my attack to distract the shadowy figure. I intended to roar in a predatory fashion, but instead squealed like a boiling kettle. The noise worked. The figure twisted its head sharply just in time to see a pint-size, red-haired Elvis hurtling in his direction.

He had time for a brief yelp. Then I crashed into him and we tumbled to the wooden floor in a tangle of thrashing limbs.

May screamed, jumping out of our path. We rolled for a few feet until a low bench halted our progress. I crawled out from underneath my suspect, who was examining his elbow and crying bitterly. Not typical arch criminal behavior.

May stepped back, then forward. "What are you doing?"

I stood, gasping, "It's me, Fletcher. He did it. All of it. We have him."

May frowned. "Fletcher. That's you? That was you at the oil tank?"

"Yes," I said urgently. "I thought April was behind everything. But I was wrong. This is the criminal right here. It's all about the talent show."

"I don't think so, Fletcher," said May. "David couldn't hurt a butterfly."

"I'm a pacifist," sobbed David, rubbing his elbow.

I thought my heart would burst with exertion and excitement. "But he was creeping toward you, dressed in black. You don't have to be a detective . . ."

"We were both rehearsing over here. David is a mime."

A mime? Oh, no.

David glared at me. "I won't be opening any invisible doors with this arm, thanks very much."

A mime. How could I have been so stupid?

A crowd was gathering. Teachers were surely on the way. Perhaps Officer Cassidy.

"Fletcher," whispered the children. "It's Fletcher Moon."

I had to go. Now.

My cover was blown. I was finished. And I knew how this would look. It would seem as though I had come here in disguise to have another go at May.

Red came to my rescue again. He elbowed through the crowd and grabbed my forearm.

"Let's go, Watson. We're on."

I allowed myself to be pulled along, though the phrase *We're on* filled me with dread. Genie and Herod were in the wings chanting the vocal exercise:

> *"Dog sees*
> *Some shoes,*
> *Dog eats,*
> *Dog poos."*

I suspected they had made up this exercise themselves.

"Come on," said Red.

"We're not warmed up," protested Genie. "Just two more dogs."

"And two more poos," added Herod, adjusting his sideburns.

Red propelled them both onstage, dragging me along.

A folk-singing trio had just finished a version of "Country Roads" and were in the middle of their bow when we tumbled onto the stage. Behind us, the other acts swarmed into the wings. My name was on everyone's lips.

Moon the lunatic is here. In disguise.

Principal Quinn arrived onstage from the opposite wing, shooting Red a look that would have petrified a minotaur. *You will pay for this later*, the look promised.

"Well, ladies and gentlemen," she announced through a whistling microphone. "In a change to the advertised program, it seems as though Red Sharkey is next, with his version of the Elvis classic 'Love Me Tender.' The stage is yours, Red, and I look forward to discussing your performance later."

Principal Quinn bowed slightly. Mockingly.

Red grinned feebly and stepped up to the microphone to a slight smattering of applause. The clapping was almost drowned out by a sea of buzzing, as muted cell phones received text messages. The word of my presence was spreading.

Red struck a pose, waiting for Genie to cue the mini-disk player on the stool behind her. A moment later, the sound of an Elvis backing track filled the hall.

"Love me tender . . ." he sang in a beautiful sultry tenor.

Genie and Herod swayed in unison behind the second mike, bumping me on both sides.

"Ooh ooh ooh," they sang.

"Oops, *ooh,* sorry," I moaned.

"Love me sweet . . ."

He never got past the second line, because hundreds of students were pulling out their cell phones. The text jumped cricket-like from phone to phone as everybody read, then passed it on to everyone in their phone book. May's words had spread through the audience like a virus.

U R not gng 2 Blve ds. 1/2 Moon is here.

I knew what was happening. I felt as though my disguise was becoming slowly transparent. Students were staring at me. Initially in disbelief, then with dawning realization as their brains ran a profile on my features. One little first-grade girl put her finger on it.

She stood slowly, still deciphering the message on her phone screen. I have always thought that six was too young for a cell phone. Now I was certain of it.

"That ugly boy," she said, pointing to me in case

anyone was in doubt as to who exactly the ugly boy was. "My phone says he's Half Moon."

I expected instant chaos. I was wrong. This was such a fantastic situation—so unusual, so exciting, that no one wanted it to end. My audience froze, willing me to speak. Principal Quinn and Officer Cassidy were the exceptions, but they were being held back by the throngs in the wings. They wouldn't be held back forever. I had ten seconds to solve this case.

The clues whirled in my head. Red was right. There was no denying it. Only one person had benefited from each and every incident, and I had been blind not to see it. The truth hit me like a series of fireworks inside my brain. Emotions and allegiances became unimportant. Truth was truth. This is the burden of the detective.

I stepped forward in a daze. Knowing something, and making others believe it are two different things. My words would mean nothing, unless they could be confirmed by the guilty party. I had to force a confession. Nothing else would save me.

I turned quickly to Herod. "I need your help," I whispered, covering the mike. "Red needs it, too."

Herod squinted at me, and the desperation in my eyes told him that this was not the time to argue.

He nodded briefly, and I whispered to him what might need to be done.

A smile lit up his little face. "It's the opposite of what I generally do."

I pulled the microphone from its stand. It came away, trailing a ribbon of duct tape. Time to face my public.

"Hello, Lock," I said, smiling a watery smile.

Beside me Herod groaned, and Genie covered her face. I glanced across at Red. He bowed, yielding the stage to me. If I didn't pull this off, all the Sharkeys were in for it, including the fake one.

Someone called from the back rows. "Is it really you, Half Moon? Are you really an obsessive-compulsive schizophrenic?"

Some people should not be allowed to watch television after nine.

"Yes, it is really me," I replied, my voice booming and hollow through the hall's speakers. "I've come here because I am innocent, and I can prove it."

The statement was met with a wall of cynicism. I felt like a lone archer trying to breach the walls of Troy. Still, no one rushed the stage. It was the kind of real-life adventure that people would never forget.

Even Principal Quinn and Officer Cassidy were hooked. They were no longer struggling to get onstage, instead they elbowed their way to a decent viewing spot. I had better deliver, and fast.

"I know you all think I'm crazy," I began, easing into it.

"Boo!" shouted an audience member.

"Get on with it!" called another.

"When is the magician coming on?" whined an elderly man in the front row. "I heard there was a magician."

Okay. Maybe a warm-up was a bad idea. Cut to the chase.

"It was all about the talent show," I proclaimed, spreading my arms wide. It was good theater. "That's why I came here tonight, to protect a particular performer from danger."

A rustle of whispers spread through the crowd. Someone was in *danger*? This just got better and better.

"It all started twelve months ago on this very stage. *Someone* got beaten very badly in this competition, and *someone* didn't like it."

I moved across the stage, and hundreds of heads swiveled to follow.

"So, let's see who was in that competition. There was Red Sharkey, the overall winner. Red shouldn't be here tonight, because he got himself suspended for supposedly assaulting me. So, as far as our criminal was concerned, Red was out of the picture."

"Which is a shame, Mama," interjected Red. "'Cause I'm purty good at whut I do."

This got a big laugh. Everyone loves a comedian.

I shot Red a disapproving look, which he naturally ignored.

"Second place went to Mercedes Sharp, for her

Britney act. But someone stole Mercedes's karaoke mini-disk, so she pulled out, presumably to concentrate on being the town gossip."

Not strictly relevant, I know. But Mercedes had been poking fun at me for years. Judging by the round of applause, I wasn't the only one she'd poked fun at.

"Johnny Riordan and Pierce Bent were third. They didn't enter this year because their DJ friend's needles were stolen. No turntables, no act."

I was making inroads. I could see a few thoughtful faces in the audience. Not many, but a few.

"Fourth place went to SeeSaw Halpin."

"SeeSaw," howled the fifth grade as one. This happened every time his name was mentioned, which was very frustrating for his teachers, and his parents, who would really prefer that everyone call him Raymond.

"But unfortunately, SeeSa . . . eh, Raymond's sister was injured this year and he was unable to continue his dance lessons. So Seesaw is out."

"SEESAW!"

"Fifth place went to Gretel Bannon. She didn't enter this year, because her babysitter, Maura Murnane, was tricked into overeating and hasn't been herself. Without Maura, Gretel has had no one to take her to recorder class."

It was starting to click with people now that what I was saying made real sense.

"Sixth was Julie Kennedy, who was not allowed to enter this year because her grades fell. Her grades fell because her after-school tutor received something nasty in the mail and left town. Six entrants for this competition, all taken out by apparently unconnected situations. Too many coincidences. Entirely too many."

"So who came next?" called a voice from the back of the hall.

The obvious question. I was hoping someone would ask it. I paused before answering. Whatever I said next would change my life. Someone I liked a lot would be hurt. Forever. For there was no chance that I was wrong. I knew who the guilty party was.

"May Devereux," I whispered into the wire mesh of the microphone head.

A collective *oooh* rose from the audience. I didn't blame them. This was good stuff for five euros.

"Fletcher, what are you saying?" May had pushed her way on to the stage. With her dance costume, blond hair, and wobbling lip, she looked the picture of innocence. I would have less trouble convincing a trekkie that Spock was an impulsive hothead. Still, I only needed to convince one person.

"Are you saying that I did all those things? Is that what you mean?"

I turned, blocking the sparkle of her costume from my vision. What I was doing was cruel, but it had to be done. This had to stop tonight.

"That's exactly what I mean, May."

She took a step to the left, her sequins glinting. "Why can't you look at me, Fletcher? Is it because you know I'm innocent?"

"Innocent?" I scoffed. "Not too innocent to set up everyone who beat you in last year's show."

"But they got me, too. My lucky costume."

"Maybe," I countered. "But you're still here."

She didn't answer. Not because she didn't have an answer, but because she was going for the innocent, hurt look.

I plowed on. May's credibility had to be torn to shreds. It was the only way this could work.

"Take a look, everyone. Lovely May Devereux. As pretty as her name. The perfect student and a doting daughter. But behind this facade is someone who will do anything to get her way. Being seventh in a competition was never going to be enough for May. After last year's humiliation, she plotted her strategy for months. It was a simple enough plan: take out everyone who finished higher than her."

May had turned so pale that she seemed almost translucent.

"So Mercedes's mini-disk is stolen, Johnny and Pierce lose their decks, the chocolate phantom visits Maura Murnane. The list goes on. But there was one problem: Master Red Sharkey. Red has already been in more trouble than May can throw at him. Red has backbone and will not be broken; his family can't be used against him. May is getting desperate, she's running out of ideas. Then one day her cousin April, who has her own scheme, hires me to track down a fictitious lock of Shona Biederbeck's hair. It was perfect."

I paused for breath. You could have heard a potato chip crunch—but didn't because this drama was more absorbing than any snack. Which is saying a lot for school kids.

"April and May set me on Red's trail like a good doggy. I get assaulted, Red gets blamed, and May is the least-likely suspect. Perfect."

May found the resolve to step forward under the lights. Her costume shimmered like a disco ball.

"You do know I'm only ten, don't you, Fletcher? And anyway, you can't prove any of this," she said with some steel behind her trembling voice.

Proof. The hole in my case. A rather significant hole. But this was all part of the plan.

"I don't need proof, because everyone in this hall knows it's true. Your life as the popular princess is over."

What I was doing was cruel. Terrible. I hated myself. I wished there was another way.

May retreated in the face of this onslaught. She mouthed my name, but no sound came out.

"You had more than most, May, but it wasn't enough. You had to have the talent show crown as well, even if it meant climbing over your own schoolmates. Some of your victims have been friends since kindergarten. How could you?"

"She didn't!" said a voice from the crowd. The outburst I had been praying for. The sound of that simple sentence was like the clanging of a victory bell. I knew, with absolute certainty, that my theory had been correct. It was as if a ghost had taken on flesh and revealed himself to the world.

"No," I said, turning to face the man who had left his seat and was standing red faced in the aisle. "She didn't. You did. Isn't that right, Mr. Devereux?"

May's father, Gregor Devereux, looked back at his seat as if he had no idea why he wasn't still in it. His eyes swiveled to meet mine, and they were the eyes of a guilty man. Everything slotted into place with the precision of a laser-cut jigsaw, and the true thrill of detection sent a shiver through my senses. For a moment everything dissolved but the truth.

Devereux pointed a finger at me. "You just . . . You just leave my little girl . . . You just shut up, you little . . ."

"Unfinished sentences," I said. "A sure sign of guilt."

No one moved. No one spoke. Mothers clamped their hands over infants' mouths.

"It took me a long time to see it," I said, stepping to the lip of the stage. "I was so stupid, for so long. It had to be you, Mr. Devereux."

"Call me Gregor," said May's father automatically.

"Everything pointed to May, because she was the one to benefit. But if she didn't do it herself, and I never for a moment believed that she did, then who would want her to benefit. *Who?* Her father, of course."

Gregor Devereux tried to laugh, but no sound came from his mouth.

"Fletcher, you're disturbed. Everybody knows it. You're a fugitive, for heaven's sake."

Reasonable enough words, but the delivery was hollow.

I pointed a rigid finger straight at his heart. "You stole the needles. You sent the package. You left the chocolate. It was all you. On a crusade to prove to the wife that walked out on you that you could raise May on your own. A pushy father who refused to accept the fact that his daughter could not dance."

"She *can* dance!" blurted Devereux. "She can. Like her mother used to. All May needs is some encouragement. A confidence booster."

"Daddy?" May was center stage now, eyes wide and wet. "Tell them it's not true. Tell me."

Gregor Devereux realized what he was saying. How close he was to a confession. He closed his eyes for a second, collecting himself. When he reopened them, they were sincere and almost merry.

"Of course it's not true," he said, smiling in

fatherly reassurance. "I care about your dancing, of course, princess. But that's all. I would never *do* anything. Never *hurt* anybody."

May was convinced. Of course she was. He was her daddy.

"There," she said to me. "I hate you, Fletcher."

My heart quailed but I forged ahead.

"May had the motive and the opportunity, but there were a few pieces of the puzzle that just didn't fit until you showed up on my radar, Mr. Devereux."

"Oh, you have *radar* now," joked Gregor, but nobody laughed.

"First there were the strange footprints left in my garden, by the one who attacked me. Giantlike prints. Then I realized that the marks were not made by feet alone, but by knee pads and toes. The kind of marks that would be made by an adult kneeling down. An adult pretending to be a child, wearing gardening pads. I see there are faint strap marks on the knees of your pants, *Gregor.* Are you wearing the same pants tonight?"

"Ridiculous," scoffed Mr. Devereux.

"Maybe," I said. "But my father uses a home-made fertilizer. An absolutely unique concoction. I am sure the police lab can match any soil from your soles to the fertilizer in our garden."

Gregor Devereux was blinking fast and sweating. His bangs flopped into his eyes and he pushed them back, flattening the hair to his head.

"Nothing," he said, appealing to the audience for support. "None of this means a thing. The delusions of a strange boy. We've all known it for years, haven't we? We've all known that little Half Moon is not quite right. A midget detective? Please."

He was right. People did think I was strange. They still do. But that didn't change the truth.

"But let's get back to Mercedes's music. The missing mini-disk. We found your footprint under her window, and there was also evidence of a frenzied search. As though the thief had lost something. But what could he have lost?"

Hundreds of chairs squeaked as the audience leaned in.

"I forgot the most basic rule of investigation: the most obvious explanation is usually the right one. The only thing you could have lost was the thing you came to find, the mini-disk that you had overheard Mercedes talk about so many times."

"Fantasy," bellowed Mr. Devereux. "Pure fantasy!"

But his blink rate jumped, as though it were wired to the power grid. I was right!

"You lost the mini-disk during the break-in. I saw the flower bed outside May's window. It was torn apart. You had no option but to return home and hope the mini-disk didn't turn up before the talent show."

My big speech had ended with a whimper rather than a bang. My entire theory was bordering on the incredible. It was a stretch. I knew it and so did everyone else. I needed a trump card, and Mr. Devereux provided it. He strode purposefully down the center aisle, vaulting onto the stage. He speared me with a withering look and grabbed the microphone. The Sharkeys were elbowed from his path. Herod stumbled at Gregor's feet, remaining there for a moment before joining his sister in the wings.

"How much more of this insanity are we supposed to stomach?" he asked. "You all know me. Frank, Seamus. We play squash together. Is any of this the least bit credible? I don't even know why I'm bothering to defend myself. Come on, honey, let's go home."

I motioned to Red, and he tossed me his microphone.

"One more thing, Mr. Devereux. The mini-disk."

Gregor blew his fuse. "What about it?" he bellowed. "Conjured it up out of thin air, have you? Give it a rest! Haven't you caused enough pain? Think of your parents."

"Those pants you're wearing, with the curious strap marks in the corduroy. Black, with plenty of pockets. Big cuffs, too. I'm guessing they are your sneaky pants. . . ."

"Work pants!" spat Gregor. He rolled his eyes. "Why am I explaining myself to you?"

I took a step closer. "If a small disk were to fall out of a person's pocket, it could easily slip into one of those cuffs. You're right-handed, so in the right cuff. If that disk were to survive the washing machine, it could still be there."

Devereux's laugh was short and sharp, like the warning bark of a territorial dog. "Get away from me, Moon. I'm not subjecting myself to a search from you."

I met his wild gaze with a steady one of my own. "Just one second to bend down. One second and everyone knows I'm a lunatic."

"Shove your second, Fletcher. And shove your accusations. I am sick of being the polite, responsible adult. I'll say what we're all thinking. Your parents have to take a firmer line with you."

May moved toward her father. He smiled triumphantly and reached out a hand. She did not take it.

"I'll show him, Daddy," she said. She knelt by his right pant cuff and quickly found the disk tucked in there.

"Oh, Daddy," she sighed, with a sorrow that squeezed my heart.

Gregor was flabbergasted. "That's impossible. That can't be. What?"

I hammered home my advantage. "There it is. The stolen disk. Explain that, *Gregor*, if you can."

May's father took the disk in a trembling hand. His face was wrinkled with incomprehension. "May, you have to believe me. I . . . this . . ." The words wouldn't come. His mouth churned uselessly for several moments until he finally blurted: "Don't you understand? I wasn't even wearing these pants that night!"

The room was silent for an instant as everyone digested the importance of this statement, then Red raised both arms to the crowd.

"Confession!" he roared, and the crowd went crazy. This was real entertainment.

"You attacked me!" I accused, through the commotion.

Gregor looked around desperately, as if he was expecting a rescue from somewhere.

"I attacked a garden gnome!" he shouted. "You came out of nowhere. I would never hurt anyone. All I wanted to do was destroy the gnome and leave Red's hurl so that he would be blamed. That's all. May, you have to believe me."

In the eye of the hullabaloo, tears dripped from Gregor's eyes as his daughter turned from him. The tears turned to ice and he took three quick steps across the stage and grabbed me by the shoulders.

"You don't know what you've done," he growled. "May is fragile. She is still recovering from her mother leaving."

I wriggled, but Gregor had me in his strong gardener's hands. Red was the first to react. He hurtled across the stage, tackling Devereux below the waist. But he was only thirteen, and Devereux was a six-foot-plus plank of fitness. Red bounced off him like a bird off a window. All the impact did was remind Devereux where he was.

"Stay back," he warned, hoisting me off the ground. "Let me think. Give me room."

I don't think now that Gregor Devereux was in his right mind on that evening. I don't think he was aware that he was dangling my legs over the orchestra pit.

Cassidy took a few steps onstage, palms raised. "Come on, Devereux. God knows none of us are fond of Half Moon, pain in the behind that he is, but you have to put the boy down before you drop him."

"In a second, Cassidy," said Devereux calmly. "I just need to find the right words, to explain things to May." He pulled a face. "Her mother will have a field day with this."

My future at this point was uncertain, and I had only myself to blame. I'd pushed a man over the edge in uncertain circumstances.

I heard something. The sharp smack of metal striking wood. The noise came again and again. Increasing in intensity until a rhythm was established.

The pressure on my shoulders eased slightly. "May," whispered Devereux.

I realized what the noise was. Dancing shoes. May was dancing. With tears streaming down her cheeks,

May Devereux was performing her competition routine to distract her own father.

Devereux was instantly transfixed. The real world was forgotten. The current crisis took a backseat to the talent competition.

"Come on, honey," he said. "Head up, back straight."

May danced like she had never done before, somehow finding coordination in her flashing feet. The noise of her tap shoes silenced the crowd as they realized that something special was happening.

Gregor's head bobbed along with the routine. "Two, three, four, five, six, seven, and heel, toe. Fingers crossed now, honey."

Gregor held his breath. The click-kick was coming. May had never managed this in her life. Tonight she did. Her legs flashed straight as rulers four feet up, heels smacking together on the descent. She finished with a deep bow.

Gregor Devereux ran across the stage, dragging me with him. He glared at the judges seated in the first row. "Well?" he demanded.

Sister Julie B. Winters, the chief judge, looked to her co-judges for support. When none came, she spoke haltingly. "Good . . . I mean *excellent* presentation. Nice technique and form. Impressive click-kick. I would say, definitely, first place. First, no doubt about it."

Gregor's face cracked with relief. A mountain of stress lifted from his shoulders. "You won, honey. We won. It was all worth it. All the practice. All the . . . everything." He turned back to the judges. "Where's the trophy? Isn't there a trophy?"

Sister Julie picked up the marble trophy at her feet and passed it into the waiting hands of Gregor Devereux.

Gregor Devereux's hands were empty and waiting to receive it, because he had cast me aside.

Cassidy should have had him, or any one of a hundred adults in the wings, but they didn't, because my mother never gave them the chance. The text of my presence had reached her cell phone from one of the mothers' circles. She had immediately jumped into the car and driven to the hall. At the exact moment Gregor dropped me, she was barging through the crowds in the wings. When Mom realized what was going on, she pulled a curtain rail sampler from her shoulder bag and charged Gregor Devereux, who had an eight-inch and eighty-pound advantage over her.

Devereux was in the act of hoisting May's trophy when a foot length of cherrywood struck him on the temple, swung with the strength of motherhood. Gregor pirouetted once, then dropped like a sack of stones.

May flung herself on his chest, sobbing.

"I'm sorry," I said to the one girl who had ever liked me. "It was the only way."

May raised her head long enough to say the words that have haunted my dreams since that night. "What my daddy did was bad," she said, her bleary eyes like dark stones underwater. "But what you did tonight was worse."

Maybe I could have persuaded her otherwise, but my mother smothered me in her arms and the moment was lost.

Now it is too late. Now she hates me for life.

Join the club.

EPILOGUE

MY NAME IS MOON. Fletcher Moon. And I'm not sure if I want to be a detective anymore.

It had been almost a month since the talent competition fiasco. It was big news for a while, thanks to over a hundred amateur video and phone recordings. I even made the national news. So much for undercover work. Not that it mattered. I was finished with investigative work. May was hurt. Wounded. I never wanted to do that to someone again. Her mother had left her and now, in a way, her father was gone, too. Gregor Devereux was no longer the shining knight that every dad should be. All because of me.

My parents read me the riot act, and watched me

so closely that I couldn't take on any cases even if I wanted to. Mom checked my room a dozen times a night to make sure that I was still here. Dad wrote a daily timetable for me, filled with menial tasks, the theory being that I would be too exhausted to even think about detection. And, of course, they confiscated my badge.

I spent my time faking the symptoms of post-traumatic stress disorder to avoid facing everyone. I walked around staring into space, hoping that nobody would try to strike up a conversation. This tactic proved successful. My sister, Hazel, was very happy with the new me, and was making a documentary on my progress.

At school, most people left me alone. Even the remains of *Les Jeunes Etudiantes* were afraid to stir up the hornets' nest.

Sergeant Murt Hourihan was the closest thing I had to an ally. He stood up to Chief Quinn, insisting that the investigation against me be scrapped. Of course Gregor Devereux is suing me for slander, but his case has about as much hope before a jury as a house of straw has before the big bad wolf. Especially since Devereux made a full confession at the police station. His lawyer advised him not to press charges against my mother for assault, as he had just been threatening her son.

Murt came over to the house when things had settled down. "How are you holding up, Sherlock?"

he asked when he had finally managed to get me alone at the kitchen table.

"Sherlock Holmes is a creation," I said sullenly. "At the end of the book, he moves on to the next adventure. I can't move on. I live here."

Murt leaned back in the chair, popping a jacket button.

"That was a nice trick, planting the mini-disk in Gregor Devereux's cuff. Lucky he didn't spot the plant."

"It was an Elvis track, from the hall sound system. Herod did it when Devereux pushed him over. We had it set up."

"Totally illegal, of course. It's entrapment."

"I don't care about procedure anymore. I'm finished with law and order."

Murt sighed. "There was once this poet fellow by the name of Keats," he stated.

Murt was full of surprises. "What about Keats?"

"Well now, young Keats was well known for immortal lines, and my own particular favorite is 'Beauty is truth, truth beauty—that is all/Ye know on earth, and all ye need to know.' Do you see what I mean?"

"I'm not sure. What do you think you mean?"

Murt spun his cap onto the kitchen table like a Frisbee. "Ah, nice to see a spark of the smart alec we all know and love. What I *think* I mean, is that truth is priceless. Or to give it the Sergeant Murt Hourihan treatment: Tell me the truth, the whole truth and nothing but the truth or go directly to jail. When you exposed Gregor Devereux, you gave everyone in that hall the gift of truth."

"May didn't see it as a gift. She hates me."

Murt snagged an apple from the fruit bowl. "Look," he said. "Life is like an apple."

I raised my head out of my hands to look at the apple. This should be good.

Murt stared at the apple for several moments, then ate it in half a dozen bites. "Okay, I can't finish that simile. But give me some credit for the Keats. Come on, I looked that up on the Internet."

"You better change your police site password," I said guiltily.

Murt gave me the eye. "Why do you say that?"

I avoided his gaze. "I guessed it. Blue Flew. Too obvious."

"Hmm. I think you're right. Anyway, better you guessing it than someone dangerous. There are people who would have a field day with that information."

I nodded listlessly.

"Come on, Fletcher. Gimme a smile. May despises you now. She blames you for what's happened. But do you really think that this is your fault? You did the right thing, however unorthodox your methods."

* * *

Truth is beauty.

It was a few weeks later, and I was sitting on my own in the lunch hall.

Life was rolling along with no regard for my personal gloom. Kids were chatting, flirting, fighting, and occasionally eating.

Didn't these people realize how depressed I was? I had turned my back on two things that were very important to me. My chosen profession and an unlikely friend. Red.

It had been awkward between us since the talent competition. We had been partners, I suppose, maybe friends. But now I was back in my own world, and he was still in his. I didn't even look much like a Sharkey anymore. The earring was gone, the fake tan had worn off, and there were only patches of red left in my hair. So maybe Half Moon wasn't tough enough to be a friend to Red Sharkey. It was a pity. I could have used a friend.

Then, as if my thoughts had summoned him, Red appeared. He slid along the opposite bench, looking as he always did: hurried, harried, and cool. His fiery hair stood in shocked stalagmites, and his freckles had multiplied in the unseasonable autumn heat.

"Half Moon," he half whispered. "I'm in trouble this time. Real trouble. I'm sunk, done for, up the creek. You have to help me."

Red Sharkey was actually asking for help. This must be serious.

"What happened? I'm not supposed to be talking to you, by the way."

Red ducked low, his chin an inch from the table-top, as though someone was watching. "Forget that. This is important. Life or death stuff. We can worry about your parents later. *You* are the only one who can help me."

I could feel eyes on me. I looked around and spotted Hazel standing by the juice vendor, pointing her video camera at me, hand on hips. Her body language was saying *You are so busted*. But then her gaze met mine and her features softened. She put away the camera and placed a hand over each eye. *See no evil*. For some reason Hazel had decided to give me a break. Maybe she could sense that I needed one.

"Hello, by the way," I said. "How's the family?"

"Good. Papa is delighted with me. A Sharkey who was genuinely innocent. Oh, and Roddy wants to be a detective now. How long that will last I don't know." He glanced up nervously, as though he half expected someone to be watching. "Now, my problem. Will you help?"

I felt a brushstroke of dread coat my stomach. "I don't know, Red. After our last case . . ."

Red slapped the table. People jumped. "Snap out of it, Half Moon. I need help. I need the truth, and the truth is your speciality. What are you going to do? Mope for the rest of your life?"

Red was right. He needed my help, and I should give it. Without selfish hesitation.

"Okay. Tell me quickly, before I chicken out."

"Excellent," said Red, grinning his pirate grin. "This is a real stumper. Someone will write books about this one someday. Last year I did some work on a country estate. A summer job for this American guy who'd inherited a title."

"Summer job. American nobleman. Okay."

It was enticing. So far, classic mystery setup. For a moment my depression lifted.

"So the American's family has this curse on it . . ."

A curse. No such thing, as far as detectives are concerned. But they can have a devastating effect on superstitious people.

"According to this curse, every lord of the manor gets done in by a . . . eh . . . fox."

I began to sniff a rodent. "A fox?"

"Yeah. Big fox. Enormous. Roams the moor sniffing for the American guy. Just dying to take a chunk out of his backside. . . ."

"Wait a second," I said, unable to swallow a smile. "You're making this up, or rather, stealing it from Arthur Conan Doyle. I believe the story you are butchering is *The Hound of the Baskervilles*."

Red was smiling back at me. "Okay. I'm not in trouble. But tell me your heart didn't start beating for the first time in a month."

I couldn't deny it. So I didn't.

"You're a detective, Fletcher. That's what you're good at."

"My dad took my badge."

Red wagged a finger at me. "Just because you don't have a badge, doesn't mean you don't *have* a badge," he said trying to sound wise. And strangely, I understood exactly what he meant.

Red cleared his throat nervously. "Anna Sewell, the girl who wrote *Black Beauty*, said that "with cruelty and oppression it is everybody's business to interfere when they see it," which means that you were dead right to stand up to Gregor Devereux. He was certainly cruelly oppressin' us."

"Have you been talking to Murt?" I asked suspiciously.

"Yes," admitted Red. "I've been helping him out with a few cases, since you've been out of action. He says that I am not as reliable as you. Well, what he actually said was that you may be thick, but I make you look like a certified genius."

"Typical Murt."

"I thought you might like to know that Ernie Boyle is back in school, so some good has come of all our meddling."

"Really?"

"Yeah, he's disgusted. Oh, and April Devereux's parents are moving her to a private boarding school in Dublin after her stay on the farm. Apparently some of her friends here were having a bad influence on her."

"That's rich."

"Tell me about it."

We sat quietly for a moment. Red was waiting for me to make a decision. I was trying to make it.

"So, are you volunteering to help with all this crime solving?"

Red was insulted. "Help? We're partners, Fletcher. Or we would be if you hadn't been ignoring me for the past month."

"I didn't know . . . It's not as if . . ."

Red winked. "Unfinished sentences. A sure sign of guilt."

"Sorry, Red. I haven't been myself. I've been trying to be someone else, but it hasn't worked out."

"We should have a name for our agency."

"*Our* agency?"

"Yes, our. You can be the boss, the brainy one. And I'll be the good-looking one who takes all the risks."

I felt my life's breath returning after a month's absence. We would have to be low profile. Work on the QT until Mom and Dad were ready for the idea. But we would be a good team. We had already broken one case wide open.

"What about Crimebusters?" Red was saying. "Or Junior B Men?"

"What?"

"Names. For our agency, remember?" Red squinted at me craftily. "You've already been thinking about this, haven't you? You already have a name. Let me guess: Moon Investigations."

I grinned at my new partner.

"You're half right," I said.

EOIN COLFER is the *New York Times* best-selling author of the Artemis Fowl series, *The Supernaturalist*, *Eoin Colfer's Legend of Spud Murphy* and *Legend of Captain Crow's Teeth*, and *The Wish List*. He lives in Ireland with his wife and two children.

To learn more about Eoin Colfer, visit his Web site at www.eoincolfer.com

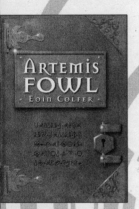
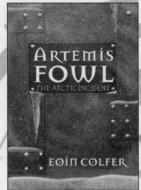

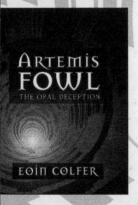
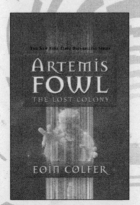